A Candlelight Ecstasy Romance®

"YOU WANT TO DOUBLE-DATE . . . ON OUR HONEYMOON?" LAURA LEE COULDN'T BELIEVE HER EARS.

"My idea of fun is two people on a honeymoon, not four!"

"Come back to bed, sweetheart. I can't convince you of anything when you're twenty feet away," Judd whispered in a seductive manner as he beckoned her with one finger.

"No way. If I slip between the sheets you'll not only have me agreeing to this bizarre plan, you'll have me thinking it was my idea to begin with. Get up, Mr. Simpson."

"Can't." He groaned. "You've worn me out."

"Complaining?" Laura teased.

"Never. I'm looking forward to a week of looking at lovely white ceilings in Florida."

"Beaches . . . not ceilings!" she contradicted playfully as she crossed the bedroom to the side of the bed and whipped back the sheet. "And . . . A-L-O-N-E!"

CANDLELIGHT ECSTASY ROMANCES

HONEYMOON

Anna Hudson

A CANDLELIGHT ECSTASY ROMANCE®

Published by
Dell Publishing Co., Inc.
1 Dag Hammarskjold Plaza
New York, New York 10017

ISBN: 0-440-13772-1

Printed in the United States of America

First printing—February 1985

Dedicated to:
Anne Gisonny,
my editor, my friend, the feisty
heroine of the publishing industry
who encourages the unexpected.
Many thanks and my heartfelt
appreciation for finding this crazy
Texan.

To Our Readers:

We have been delighted with your enthusiastic response to Candlelight Ecstasy Romances®, and we thank you for the interest you have shown in this exciting series.

In the upcoming months we will continue to present the distinctive, sensuous love stories you have come to expect only from Ecstasy. We look forward to bringing you many more books from your favorite authors and also the very finest work from new authors of contemporary romantic fiction.

As always, we are striving to present the unique, absorbing love stories that you enjoy most—books that are more than ordinary romance. Your suggestions and comments are always welcome. Please write to us at the address below.

Sincerely,

The Editors
Candlelight Romances
1 Dag Hammarskjold Plaza
New York, New York 10017

CHAPTER ONE

"You want to double-date . . . on our honeymoon?"

A high note of "you've got to be kidding" raised her normally low, husky voice to the peak of its range. Who in their right mind would want to take another couple along on their honeymoon? Laura Lee Mason couldn't believe her ears.

"Why not? We aren't going to stay in the same hotel room. It's their honeymoon, too. Mac and Vanessa are just going to share the expenses of driving to Florida." Judd pulled the sheet up to his chest as though it could protect him from the disbelief in his fiancée's tone.

"In my car, I suppose?"

Judd yawned, stretched his arms outward, then folded them behind his head. His eyes shone with a dark brilliance as they watched Laura Lee lift her copper-colored hair from beneath the lapel of her short pink robe and swing it forward over her shoulder. "Wouldn't it be more fun to drive in your convertible?"

"My idea of fun is two people on a honeymoon, not four!"

"Come back to bed, sweetheart. I can't convince you of anything when you're twenty feet away," Judd whispered in a seductive manner as he beckoned her with one finger.

Laughing, Laura Lee shook her head, a movement that flung her hair back over her shoulders. Her smoky gray eyes brimmed with mirth. "No way. If I slip between the sheets, you'll not only have me agreeing to this bizarre plan, but have me thinking it was my idea to begin with. Get up, Mr. Simpson."

"Can't," he groaned. "You've worn me out."

"Complaining?" Laura Lee said teasingly.

"Never. I'm looking forward to a week of looking at lovely white ceilings in Florida."

"Beaches, not ceilings!" she said, playfully contradicting him as she crossed the bedroom to the side of the bed and whipped back the sheet. "And . . . A-L-O-N-E!" she added, spelling the word out.

"White ceilings . . . T-O-G-E-T-H-E-R!" Judd Simpson argued. He reached up, grabbed Laura Lee, and pulled her across his chest. "Where's the girl who insisted we double-date the first night we went out?"

"That was to protect me from a lecherous sex maniac."

Chuckling, she ran one long pink fingernail over the dark masculine hairs covering his broad chest. As Judd reciprocated by following the deep V of her robe, the flesh beneath his fingertips sent an electrical impulse along the same line. His hand slipped inside her garment to knead her soft breasts.

Laura Lee feared she would lose this confrontation as she had others. Judd could invite all two hundred guests attending their wedding reception to their honeymoon, and she wouldn't object as long as he stroked and loved her.

Her fingers splayed as they framed his darkly tanned features. They had been engaged for more than a year, but she never tired of gazing at his chiseled, handsome face. She brushed the natural arch of his dark eyebrow with her forefinger. Judd closed his eyes, smiling. A double row of dark lashes fanned downward.

"You have a gray hair," Laura said. "Shall I pull it out?"

"Nope. I grew it especially for tonight. You've kept me waiting too long." His lips tilted upward. "I'm cultivating a gray streak as my souvenir for being patient. Thought I'd be bald before you set the wedding date."

Lightly pinching his cheek brought his velvet brown eyes open. Lines of laughter edged the corners of his mouth. Judd Simpson had that special talent of smiling with his entire face. It was as though the bright, fun-loving inner core of his personality exuded for everyone to see.

"We couldn't afford to get married," Laura Lee halfheartedly argued, wishing she had agreed to elope a year ago.

"So says the accountant," her impatient bridegroom retorted. "I'd live in a tent and love it as long as you shared my sleeping bag."

"Winters in Kansas City are too snowy to camp out," she protested, returning his smile.

At the moment, held closely against his chest, listening to the strong thud of his heartbeat, Laura Lee wondered how she had managed to postpone the wedding until they had a small two-bedroom house furnished and enough money to pay for the wonderful formal wedding she had dreamed of as a child. *A June bride,* she thought happily . . . with all the frivolous trimmings every girl dreams of.

The Masons insisted upon paying for the reception, but Laura Lee refused to let her parents bear the entire financial burden of a big wedding. Although they could swing a modest celebration, with her younger sister still in college and her younger brother graduating from high school, the huge shebang she and Judd's folks wanted would have put a severe strain on their budget.

Judd's parents, the Simpsons, offered to foot the bill, but Laura didn't think starting off a marriage in debt to her in-laws was a good idea. In fact, since they would have preferred Judd marry someone else—anyone else—she knew she'd be eating wedding cake for the rest of her life if they paid for it! Finally, a compromise had been agreed upon: Laura Lee's parents would pay for the reception; she would be responsible for any other expense.

To Laura Lee the risks of getting married and ending up in the divorce court lessened when the couple made their vows publicly in front of their combined friends and relatives. And like most young women, she wanted a lifetime commitment. If Judd Simpson truly loved her, he would set aside his impetuous determination to marry quickly for the solid foundation of getting their marriage off to a good start. And to Laura, the best start entailed a large wedding, money in the bank account, and a furnished dream home.

Perhaps, as Judd often stated, she was romantically old-fashioned, but she knew what she wanted and planned accordingly. What could insure future happiness more than two people in love having a big June wedding and honeymooning in Florida? Laura's grin spread. With the logic of a bookkeeper tallying up columns of mathematical notations, she knew everything would be wonderful once she convinced Judd that sharing their honeymoon was out of the question.

"Love me?" Judd whispered into the thickness of her flame-colored sweet-smelling hair.

"Devotedly."

"State nickname," he demanded lightly.

Their inside joke made Laura Lee laugh. Missouri's nickname, Show Me State, substituted for "Prove it." Since they both could be mulishly stubborn, they often laughed over the traits of native Missourians. Kidding each other, they had decided her assertiveness and his determination could be directly related to the Missouri water both of them drank.

"With this?" Laura Lee asked as she planted noisy kisses up his chest to the cleft in his chin. "I thought you were worn-out."

"Did I say that?" He wrapped his arms around her slender waist and pulled her closer. "Temporary insanity. Took me months to persuade the double-date lady to share my life . . . and my bed."

Laura Lee felt her cheeks flush. "You wouldn't want me any other way, would you?"

Judd sighed contentedly. "Unh-unh. There's something wonderful about knowing you've never shared yourself with another man as you have with me. Makes me special, doesn't it?"

"You are special." Grinning impishly, she

added, "Persuasive silver-tongued devil, aren't you?"

"Had to be. Here I'd been enjoying the carefree, lust-filled, swinging single life, playing poker with the guys, and who do I fall in love with? A virgin!"

"Complaining?" She kissed first one side of his mouth, then the other.

"Not now, but the employees of the restaurant did complain about their growling, snarling boss. Men aren't built for abstention." A wicked light entered his brown eyes. The palms of both his hands sensually cupped her hips into the cradle of his pelvic bones. "And neither are certain ex-virgins."

"Ex-virgins about to be married," she said in stipulation. "Everyone agrees sex without commitment is—"

"Great!" Judd hooted, lightly squeezing the rounded flesh beneath his hands.

"Judd!"

"Laura Lee!" he mimicked. "Before the vows are exchanged, sex is great anytime, anyplace, anyhow."

"Not for a woman. Not for me," she contended. "You're speaking out of both sides of your mouth. First you say you're glad I was a virgin; now you're saying there isn't any difference between me and a woman who has graced every bed in fifty states!" His male logic eluded

17

her. She remembered her mother's pointed question "Why buy the cow when the milk is free?" Wise women knew the value of a limited commodity.

"No, love. What I'm saying is: Men enjoy sex for the sake of pure pleasure. It's great." Seeing the frown mar her forehead, he swiftly added, "But with you it's the greatest!"

"What if it weren't great? Would you still marry me?" she asked in an effort to prove her reasoning.

Judd moved his hands to her ribs and wriggled them across her ticklish area. When he had her giggling and squirming, he paused, then soundly kissed her curved lips. "I'm not going to argue with the state debating champion. There's only one way to win an argument with you."

After rolling her beneath him, he began using his personal brand of persuasion, which penetrated through any verbal barrier she could erect.

Within seconds Laura Lee completely forgot about the male logic of making love to anything female as well as Judd's idea about doubling on their honeymoon. She closed her eyes and enjoyed the sensations Judd created with his lips, tongue, and hands. He kissed her as though their lips had been separated for years instead of for moments.

18

How he managed to untie her belt she didn't know, or care, but the exquisite path his fingers blazed aroused the desire she had only for him: her lover, her soon-to-be-husband. She was twenty-six, and she couldn't explain why in the middle of the eighties she had "saved herself" for the man she would marry. It wasn't that she hadn't been curious about sex; she had been. And it certainly wasn't for lack of opportunity. The self-imposed double-date policy had kept her from temptation.

Upon reflection, regardless of Judd's views, she didn't regret having him as her only lover. At other times, when her mind wasn't distracted by Judd's lips gently sipping at the tips of her breasts, she had wondered how a man would feel if the woman he had slept with said, "Sorry, Jack. Bill, Ralph, and George do it better." Wasn't that a risk a woman—or a man—took? She didn't want to know how Bill, Ralph, and George performed. No man could love her the way Judd did. Of that she was certain.

Laura Lee planned on merging her life with Judd. He would be her mate for life, not for just one night.

As his lips teased, Laura Lee clutched him tightly against her chest. Fingers twining in his dark, straight hair, she was reaching out for Judd to caress her entire body with his loving fingertips. She arched her back to communicate the growing tautness between her thighs.

Each time they made love, Judd watched her response. The excitement he generated in Laura Lee intensified his own pleasure. Her skin quivered beneath his tender ministrations. Although they had shared the intimacies of love previously, he stroked and caressed her until she willingly parted her legs, inviting, enticing him to explore the world of ecstasy.

Regardless of what he had said, Judd knew making love to her was unique. No other woman could excite him the way she could. No other woman had made him care whether or not it was as good for her as it was for him. Maybe selfishness had been a quality of his love-making before Laura Lee, but now all he knew for certain was that he wanted her to be more than a fleeting memory. At thirty years of age he had sown his wild oats. The harvest had left a craving for something he found with her. Love. It was love that made the difference.

Laura Lee shyly touched him. Her hand slid over his back, side, and hip as he brushed against the outside of her thigh. A low groan passed through his parted lips when her fingers curled around him. Judd had taught her to enjoy the visual as well as the tactile sensations. No longer did she squeeze her eyes shut, but there remained an element of innocence in her attempts to please him.

He watched her gray eyes soften with passion, taking on the burnished depth of antique silver as the black pupil expanded with hunger. There would be years to tutor her in the verbal language of love. For now, building trust, building desire were enough. She was an eager pupil. Once they were married and she felt secure, they could experiment.

Slowly he covered her, entered her. Her eyes widened, then lowered into a heavy-lidded, passion-filled gaze. This was his one and only love, the only woman he had proposed to, the woman he intended to live with the rest of his life. She would learn to meet his demands; he had learned to restrain himself from unleashing the full depth of his passion. Her inhibitions would flee once they were married. And he knew that soon there would come a time when she'd shout out his name in ecstasy as they made love.

Laura Lee bit back the urge to murmur his name repeatedly, to tell him of her love. Judd had certain ideas about what a woman should and shouldn't do. Would he be shocked if she were as assertive in the bedroom as she was in the office? She matched his tempo. He didn't grab, shout, pound, and thrust. He treated her as though she were as fragile as a tender rosebud.

He cherished her, pleased her with gentleness, respected her inexperienced limitations.

Afterward she cuddled into the cradle of his arm while their breathing slowed to a normal rate. There were questions she wanted to ask. But according to the articles she had read, immediately after making love wasn't the time. *When is the time?* she wondered. *Over the breakfast table?* Or should she wake Judd up in the middle of the night to pick his brain for information? There never seemed to be a right time.

Too bad they couldn't use the same approach the accounting firm used: Gather the information; tally the numbers; complete the audit; then make recommendations. Inwardly Laura Lee laughed. She wasn't a fool. The male ego of Judd Simpson would be crushed flatter than a French crepe if she got out of the bed and began scribbling down a list of questions.

There wasn't anyone she could ask. Her mother probably suspected she "slept" with Judd but certainly wasn't going to condone it by holding a family conference. She couldn't talk to Kathleen, her sister. Heaven forbid! Her parents would disown her if she hadn't set a good example for her younger sister. Secretly she wondered if Kathy knew the answers. Thanks to a signing of the virgins' pact between her and her best friend, Lynda, she couldn't ask her either.

When you can't ask your lover, or your mother, or your best friend, she pondered, *whom do you ask?* Laura Lee chuckled. *A stranger on the street?*

"Happy?" Judd inquired when he heard her laugh.

"Mmmmmm. Delectably contented."

"You don't really mind Mac and Vanessa's going along, do you?"

"Unh-unh." She agreed sleepily. Right now, enveloped in the glow of love, she wouldn't care if both their families joined them in Florida!

Judd grinned and kissed her forehead. "I knew you'd go along with the plans. Vanessa will call you tomorrow. . . ."

Laura Lee didn't hear anything else. His words were a deep baritone lullaby.

The next day after work Laura Lee rushed up her steps when she heard the telephone ringing on the other side of the locked door.

"Don't hang up," she muttered once she had inserted her key and twisted the knob.

The way the whole day had gone she was probably going to get to the phone the moment the caller disconnected. Mentally she ticked off a list of whose call she was about to miss. Couldn't be Judd. He had called earlier at work to tell her he had to tend bar in his dad's restaurant because the regular bartender was sick. On

Monday nights her parents played bridge, so it couldn't be them. Her boss never called her at home.

"Hello?" she gasped as she tossed her purse onto the sofa.

"Hi, Laura. Vanessa Cranfield here. There's been a change of plans."

"What plans?"

"The honeymoon plans," Vanessa explained as though she were talking to a dim-witted child. "We aren't going to Florida."

Laura grinned. "Gee, that's too bad. Where are you and Mac going?"

"The four of us are going to the Ozarks."

Knees buckling, Laura Lee sank onto the sofa, smashing the contents of her purse. "Oh?"

"Well, it's like this, kiddo. I can't miss a whole week of work, and since Mac and Judd arranged for us to make this a foursome, we'll have to go someplace close."

"But . . . " Laura Lee began to protest.

"Should be fun, don't you think? Who would ever think old college roommates would wind up honeymooning together?"

"It is rather mind-boggling."

"Yep. Mac is tickled to death. He's already oiling up the fishing equipment and getting the water skis ready."

"I don't fish or water ski," Laura Lee grumbled.

"But Judd loves to do both. You aren't going to be one of those women who stifle their husbands' hobbies by being a stick-in-the-mud, are you?"

Laura Lee bristled. "Stifle Judd?" *Strangle maybe, never stifle.*

"I keep telling Mac you aren't the prim and proper woman he thinks you are," Vanessa said confidently. "You're probably a real blast when you let loose."

"I have been known to have explosive moments," Laura replied sarcastically. *And one of them is going to occur about thirty minutes from now,* she silently vowed.

"Well, kiddo, I knew you'd be a sport. Don't want to ruin the big wedding by having a missing bridegroom, do you?"

Back molars grinding, a nasty retort on the tip of her tongue, she answered sweetly, "We're looking forward to attending your wedding Thursday."

"Not the big splash you're having, but I understand where you're coming from. When you've been a little fish in a big pond all your life, I guess you need to see your name in the society pages."

Good breeding kept Laura Lee from telling Vanessa where she put the society page when she saw the Cranfield name in print. Unwittingly her eyes drifted toward the canary cage.

Mac's future bride seldom missed a chance to rub her nose in the Mason "middle-class" upbringing. Lining the birdcage was a mild form of poetic justice.

"We're happy with the wedding plans," Laura Lee responded, making an effort to keep sharp, hissing noises out of her voice.

"Judd wanted to elope, didn't he? He's such an impetuous, ardent lover!"

"I'll tell him you remember him kindly," Laura Lee ground out the words. "Oh, dear, someone is at the door. Bye." She didn't wait for a response; she crashed the phone down.

Slowly Laura Lee began counting from 100 backward. "Ninety-nine, ninety-eight, ninety-seven, ninety-six, ninety-five, ninety-four . . ." Counting generally gave her time to cool her redhead's temper off, but this time she knew it wouldn't help.

What was happening to all those beautiful honeymoon plans she and Judd had made? Nobody double-dated on a honeymoon! And now not only was she going with a woman who looked down her patrician nose at her, but she wasn't even getting to go to Florida! *Mac and Vanessa can afford to go anyplace on earth, and where are they going? To the Ozarks. With me!*

Laura Lee picked up the phone and punched in the numbers as though they were part of Vanessa's face.

"Judd Simpson, please. This is Laura Lee." Tapping her toe on the carpet, she impatiently waited.

"Laura Lee, I'm sorry, but Judd isn't here," Joe, the bartender, said. "Did he tell you he would be working tonight?"

"I thought he did," she replied. "He called while I was working. Maybe I misunderstood him."

"He left before I came in at four. Do you want to talk to his mother?"

"No . . . thanks. I'm certain it's an innocent mixup. By the way, how are you feeling?"

"Feeling? Fine. Am I supposed to be sick?"

Lips thinning into a straight line, Laura Lee felt her stomach flop. Judd certainly wasn't tending bar for the "sick" bartender. Where was he? What was he doing? But more important, why had he intentionally lied?

"Of course not. There is a flu bug going around the office, and I wondered if any of the restaurant employees were ill," she explained with a weak laugh. She didn't want a restaurant employee to spread the rumor that the boss was lying to his prospective bride.

"Hasn't hit here. But it was nice of you to be concerned."

"Joe, if Judd comes in, would you have him call me?"

"Sure. We're all looking forward to the wedding reception. The back room is stacked with wedding gifts."

"Lovely," Laura Lee distractedly responded. "Bye, Joe."

Feeling as though she had been double-whammied in the stomach, Laura Lee folded her arms around her waist. How could these disasters be happening three days prior to her wedding? These were supposed to be joy-filled days.

The clasp of her purse dug into her upper thigh. Not being a person given to heartfelt sighs, she yanked the purse out from under herself and opened the catch. When she saw the white creamy insides of the Twinkie she hadn't had time to eat at lunch squashed against her checkbook, pocket calculator, and pens, she took it as an omen of the immediate future.

"Don't be a pessimist," she said aloud, chiding herself. "Everything is explainable or changeable." *Sure it is,* a sarcastic inner voice replied. *You thought Vanessa's call was a disaster until you found out Judd had lied, didn't you?*

Laura Lee jackknifed off the sofa and strode to the kitchen with her mashed purse. "Nothing and nobody is going to impose Murphy's Laws on me," she vowed aloud forcefully. "I'm getting married only once, and it's going to be a day to remember!"

CHAPTER TWO

"But, sweetheart, you agreed to let Mac and Vanessa come along, and Mac has made reservations for all of us at Tan-Tar-A," Judd protested later the same evening on the phone after he had returned to the restaurant and received her urgent message.

"Terrific. You and Mac can view those lovely ceilings. I am not, I repeat, not changing the original plans. Mac and Vanessa are not going anywhere with me on my honeymoon! I'm going to Florida! Got it?"

Laura sank down onto the sofa cushion ready to battle tooth and nail to have her honeymoon her way. Since Judd wasn't here to muddle her determination with kisses, hugs, and reassurances, she should be able to talk him into reverting to the original plan.

"Maybe I'd better come over and convince you everything is copacetic."

"Everything is lousy when it should be wonderful. I can't believe you arbitrarily changed our honeymoon plans."

"Not arbitrarily. You agreed to let them ride along with us. What's the big deal where we go?"

"The big deal is . . . you solve every problem we have in bed. With me capitulating."

Judd chuckled. "All the cartoons show the woman displaying her purchases of diamond rings, fur coats, and designer dresses afterward. Sexism in reverse? Why don't I leave the restaurant now and test out this revolutionary idea of a man's using sex as a weapon?"

"Speaking of the restaurant, how is dear Joe? I certainly hope his illness isn't terminal," Laura Lee gibed at Judd sweetly.

"You talked to Joe, didn't you?" Exasperation lay heavily in the question.

"Why, sweetheart, are you telling me Joe is perfectly healthy?"

"You'll have to trust me sometime, might as well start now," Judd replied, obviously unwilling to reveal his whereabouts. "You're suffering from prewedding nervous jitters. What happened to your sense of humor?"

Laura Lee paused. Throughout the past year they both had enjoyed laughing at the ridiculous situations they found themselves in. But she couldn't laugh now. Taking Vanessa anywhere wasn't funny.

"This isn't the way I dreamed the week before our wedding would be. Maybe thirty years from now I'll be able to chuckle as our children march down the aisle, but right now—"

"Don't worry about anything, sweetheart. It's only a three-hour drive to the lake. Once we get there, we'll stay at separate hotels."

Laura Lee wanted to tell him about the snide remarks Vanessa had expressed earlier. Somehow she knew Judd would interpret the altercation as a women's petty squabble. Vanessa could charm the birds out of the trees when men were around. And shoot the feathers off them once the men had turned their backs.

"Judd, how do you manage to make the entire situation sound reasonable? Couldn't we go ahead with our Florida plans?"

"I didn't think you'd object so strenuously, or I wouldn't have made any changes." Lowering his voice, he said coaxingly, "It isn't as though we made hotel reservations that we have to cancel. What difference does it make where the ceilings are?"

"There aren't any beaches in Missouri," she complained, letting her disappointment show.

"Osage Beach at the lake has to have a beach," Judd said. "How about going along with the switch in plans if I swallow my pride and tell you where I was earlier?"

"The way things have gone today, I'm not

31

certain I want to know." Laura Lee forced herself to laugh. "You were probably with some gorgeous brunette."

"The salesman was dark-headed . . . but definitely far from gorgeous. I was buying your wedding gift."

Laura Lee glanced at the inch space between the bottom of the closed bedroom door and the floor and was certain she could walk upright into the bedroom without opening the door. Here she had spent the last few hours picturing him committing a multitude of nefarious deeds while in actuality Judd had spent the time shopping for a surprise wedding gift.

"I truly wasn't checking up on you. Vanessa called to inform me of the change in plans, and I wanted to discuss them with you."

Don't tell him she intimated they were having an affair, she silently cautioned herself. *That's playing right into her hands when she is making up the rules as she goes along.*

"Not jealous? You're wounding my ego," Judd said kiddingly. "A woman is supposed to be infuriated when a man tells her he is working late and she finds out he isn't."

Laughing, she confessed, "I pictured you having a prewedding final fling."

"A man sends bouquets of roses to cover his guilt, sweetheart. Has the florist arrived at your door?"

"No, but I'll file that information away for fu-ture reference," she said kiddingly.

"Believe me, you have nothing to worry about on that score. I have all the woman I can handle. As Paul Newman says, 'Why eat hamburger out when you can have steak at home?' "

"You hate steak, remember?" Laura Lee couldn't help tweaking his nose. Since he had been reared in the restaurant business and eaten a million and one steaks, he had professed to preferring a beating over being served a piece of sirloin.

"You're twisting my meaning again. Guess the only solution is to discuss this issue in bed."

Primly, making every effort to keep the laughter out of her voice, she retorted, "Mr. Simpson, you have a one-track mind."

"If I were there, I'd kiss that saucy little mouth of yours until you were speechless."

"Promises, promises."

"Okay, sweetheart, pucker up, I'm on my way."

"Judd, no! It's ten o'clock, and I have a million and one things to do."

"I'm kidding, love. Much as I'd like to be with you, I have a king-size wedding reception to prepare for. Not many men help prepare the food for their own receptions, huh?"

"While you're whipping up delicacies, think about the poor woman who has to compete with a fantastic chef each time she prepares a meal. Hot dogs and beans aren't going to be acceptable, right?"

"Anything I don't have to fix is a gourmet feast!"

"That's what you say before the wedding. How about ten years down the road?"

"As long as you abide by the two rules we've already established—no steak and no frozen dinners—there shouldn't be any problems."

Laura Lee could hear someone talking to him in the background. Business took priority over lighthearted conversation. Patiently she waited for Judd to take care of the problem.

"Customer complaint about the shrimp cocktail. Sorry about the interruption, love. Incidentally, has your mother arranged for the friend who is baking the wedding cake to have it delivered early Saturday morning?"

"Mother is personally supervising setting it up," she said reassuringly.

"Fine. The bakery we do business with is still perturbed about our not accepting its gift of a five-tier wedding cake."

"I'd rather offend the bakery than my mother."

Their conversation was interrupted again by a flustered waiter.

"I have to placate a customer. Love you," he said to her.

"Love you . . ." The line disconnected before her whispered "too."

Laura Lee replaced the phone with mixed emotions. Had she agreed to double-date on their honeymoon and switch the destination? Mentally she tried to change the image of the two of them strolling down a sandy beach hand in hand to one of her being dragged behind a boat on two splinters while Judd, Mac, and Vanessa laughed at her awkwardness from inside the ski boat.

That's what you get for not trusting him. The devil inside her goaded her. *You should have known the little white lie he told wasn't important. Now you've bargained yourself into a double-date honeymoon. Learn anything?*

"Yeah," she answered out loud, "how to wreck my honeymoon with my own mouth. I should have taken a stronger stand. I should have screamed and yelled and kicked my feet. I should have shouted *no, no, no!*"

Why didn't I? she pondered. Was there a smidgen of truth in Vanessa's gibe about her being willing to do anything to get Judd to the altar? Laura Lee punched her balled fist against her open palm.

Self-deception wasn't part of her psychological makeup. Her mathematical mind didn't allow for inaccurate computations. Analytically she should be able to total up the information logically and come up with the right answer, but she couldn't. Not this time. The simple equation "One and one makes two" had been changed to "One and one makes four." Four people on her honeymoon instead of two. Couldn't Judd see that didn't make sense?

"We're only going to ride to the Ozarks together," she said aloud. "The men will be there, so Vanessa will be on her best behavior."

Certain she would have to repeat the statement fifty times before she believed it, she shook her head with regret. How had her other friends managed to have sane wedding plans without any hitches? If all couples faced the fuss and bother, nobody would plan a big wedding.

Maybe we should have eloped, Laura Lee mused. They had considered it when Judd pushed the sexual issue. He had suggested a secret ceremony to legitimize their lovemaking, followed by the big wedding she had dreamed of. She chuckled aloud when she remembered driving to an adjoining country to get a marriage license. After using their fingers to walk through the Yellow Pages, they had been unable to find a minister who would marry them under such a "clandestine" an arrangement.

Stubbornly she had insisted upon the huge wedding. Laughing at the absurdity of being unable to get secretly married, they had tumbled into bed and relieved the frustrations that had been building over the months they had dated. With or without the marriage vows, loving Judd was the most exhilarating experience Laura Lee had ever experienced. And it had only gotten better with time.

When they announced their wedding plans, the easy flow of their relationship immediately changed. During the time they dated they had discussed everything from world politics to whether or not you had to be buried in a casket after being cremated. She remembered laughingly telling Judd she would leave all the major decisions up to him like: should the United States go to war and who the astronaut on the next space flight should be. And she would make the minor decisions: where they should live, how they should budget their money, and so forth.

They were best friends.

But once they had set the date, friends, family, and business acquaintances began adding input. Everything from where the wedding would be held to the wedding reception to who would bake the cake to who would be the photographer, florist, and dressmaker became a major issue to squabble over.

And here we are in the final stages, and what happens? Our friends throw a kink into the plans! It's a good thing you can't get divorced before you get married.

The thought sobered Laura Lee. Marriage is forever. Large weddings, ones to which all the friends and relatives are invited, are supposed to be the concrete base of a sturdy foundation.

"Maybe I do have the prewedding jitters," Laura Lee muttered as she wrapped her arms around her waist.

Rising to her feet, she knew the best cure for nervous energy was to get busy and keep busy. There weren't going to be any other alterations in the plans. Everything would go smoothly from here on out if she managed to fill the hours actively.

Laura Lee walked into the spare bedroom, where her worktable was filled with tubes of oil paints and a half-finished project she was making for Judd. She picked up her paint-smeared smock and slipped into it. Nothing relaxed her the way painting did. And this truly was a labor of love.

The gift she had been working on was their engraved wedding invitation embedded in six layers of glass with each piece of glass having swirls of moss green ribbons and yellow roses. Laura Lee was pleased with the overall effect of her brushstrokes, which gave the illusion of pressed flowers. Framed, the layered glass picture would be a memento they would always have to cherish.

She glanced at their engagement picture

mounted in a matching frame. A friend of her father's had been hired as their photographer. And their engagement picture, which had appeared in the local papers, had been attractive enough for Judd's parents to stop their grumblings about their not using the city's top wedding photographer. His parents hadn't made any secret out of what they called a champagne wedding on a beer budget.

Shrugging the unpleasant thought aside, Laura Lee began putting the finishing touches on the top pane of glass. Mentally she checked off the remaining items on her wedding preparations list. Tomorrow the two bridesmaids and the maid of honor would try on their dresses. She'd call the florist to make certain the flowers were being prepared for the hurricane lamps at the church pews. And she'd call her mother's friend to make certain the cake would arrive on schedule. Nothing else would be left to chance.

Concentrating on the fine brushstrokes of white to highlight the tiny yellowish bud, she hunched closer to her work. This had to be finished this evening or the paints wouldn't have time to dry thanks to the Kansas City humidity.

More than an hour later Laura Lee sighed contentedly as she viewed her finished artwork. The phone rang, setting off a shrill warning button in her psyche. It was almost midnight. Who in the world would be calling so late? She ran out of the workroom back to the living room and picked up the phone. "Hello?"

A mixture of gulping and sniffing came over the wire.

"Who is this?" Laura Lee asked. A tight ball of fear began winding itself in the pit of her stomach.

"Me," a choked-up, tear-filled voice replied. "I can't come to the wedding."

"Lynda? Kathy? Colleen?" Laura Lee asked.

"It's me. Colleen. I'm in the hospital in Tulsa," she said, sobbing.

"What happened? Are you okay?"

"Noooooo," her maid of honor wailed into the receiver.

"Calm down, Colleen," Laura Lee said soothingly. "Everything is going to be fine."

Inane words of comfort flowed reassuringly from Kansas City to Tulsa. Colleen blubbered incoherently about being operated on in less than an hour for an emergency appendectomy. Any thought of the repercussions for Laura Lee fled. Colleen had a phobia about hospitals. Laura Lee remembered her having had a severe case of the flu in college and refusing to go to the infirmary.

"They're going to give me shots and put me under!" Colleen sounded scared to death, certain she'd never survive the operation. "And I'll miss the wedding! If I get out of here"—she hiccuped loudly into the phone—"you're going to kill me!"

"No, I'm not," Laura Lee stated firmly. "You know your health is more important than being in a wedding. Do you want me to fly down there?"

"Yes! No! No!" Colleen answered, confused. "Yes, I want you here, but then the bride *and* the maid of honor will be missing. No, you get married," Colleen pleaded plaintively, "but you have to promise not to miss your trip to Florida because of my funeral."

"Nothing is going to happen to you, Colleen. Don't be negative!" This wasn't the time to burden her friend with her honeymoon problems.

"I'm supposed to look forward to dying?" she wailed. "Only the good die young! Hey, give me the phone back," she shouted.

Laura Lee could hear a nurse shushing Colleen, telling her she had agreed to let her make the phone call if it didn't upset her further.

"Hello? This is Nurse Shelly. We have to get Colleen ready for surgery."

"Is there anything I can do? She's so scared!"

"Your friend will be just fine. Don't worry," the nurse said reassuringly in professional tones.

"Can I call to find out how she is?"

"Certainly. Why don't you call the desk first thing in the morning? This is routine surgery. We don't expect any complications."

41

Colleen shouted in the background, "Don't believe them. That's what they tell everybody!"

"Can I talk to her again?" Laura Lee asked.

"Her mother is here. We'll take good care of her. Good-bye."

The line was disconnected before she could protest. She hung the phone up. The people at the hospital had their hands full trying to placate Colleen. They didn't need an incoherent friend badgering them at the same time.

Distressed, Laura Lee shook her head and walked into the kitchen. She took a glass out of the cabinet, opened the refrigerator, and poured herself a big slug of orange juice.

"Ought to be whiskey," she whispered aloud.

Murphy's Law: Just when you think nothing else can go wrong, sure enough, it does.

"What else can go wrong?" she asked herself with a feeling of doom approaching swiftly.

She chugalugged the juice down. Glancing out the kitchen window, she wished Judd would appear with a ladder and carry her away from all this. Getting married had to be the hardest thing she had ever done in her life!

CHAPTER THREE

The morning of the big day dawned, accompanied by an unexpected heat wave. Low, black-bottomed clouds hovered over the rooftops ominously. The threat of drenching summer showers and the increased humidity had Laura Lee perspiring as she crawled out of bed.

"It didn't rain on Mac and Vanessa's parade," she grumbled, bemoaning the fates.

Optimistically she hoped, for once, the weatherman was right in his forecast. By evening the clouds and thunderstorms were supposed to be out of the area. The old saying "If you don't like the weather in Kansas City, stick around for five minutes, and it will change" gave her hope.

Things were looking up if she discounted the weather. Colleen had come through the operation with flying colors. The best man who was supposed to be her partner had also agreed to be an usher. The dress rehearsal for the wedding had gone smoothly. The bridesmaids' dresses had arrived. True, the wrong bodices had been on the wrong full-length skirts, but that wouldn't have been a problem if Lynda hadn't been built like Dolly Parton, and Kathy along the lines of Brooke Shields.

"Too much on one end and not enough on the other," the dressmaker had commented nonchalantly. Ripping tool in hand, she busily snipped the basting thread and reassured the three giggling women that the right tops would be on the right bottoms in time for a final fitting later in the day. And they were.

Laura Lee walked over to the Chantilly lace-covered bridal gown carefully hung on the closet door. The gown was beautiful, with its old-fashioned high neck, long, pointed sleeves, and two-foot train. Seed pearls sewn on by hand graced the exquisite bodice. Her fingers lightly traced the satin piping at the waist, which formed a sharp point in front. It was pleasing to the touch and the eye.

A bridal veil, made of layer after lengthening layer of the sheerest chiffon attached to a silk crown of orange blossoms and white satin shoes completed her ensemble. It was everything she had dreamed of as a child.

Closing her eyes, she could envision the proud look on her father's face and the broad smile Judd would give her when each of them saw her in her finery. Her mother would shed silent happy tears.

With a gentle smile on her lips, she remembered the conversation she and her father had had the previous day. Unexpectedly he had dropped in after work. Prepared for another dreadful shock, Laura Lee knew her hands had clenched in fear because later there were small half-moon-shaped scratches on her palms. She heard him reassuring her that nothing had gone wrong; he just wanted to have a father-daughter talk before the wedding.

Laura Lee hugged him, tucked her hand into the crook of his elbow, and ushered him into the living room. He looked so solemn, so sad.

"You don't have to get married," he blurted. "If you aren't happy living alone, you can always move back in with us."

Totally shocked by the pronouncement, Laura Lee stared at him as though he had recently grown a purple beard.

"I love Judd, Dad. I don't have to get married; I want to marry him." Did he think she was pregnant? At twenty-six she wasn't that naïve or that stupid.

Her dad sank back into the cushion, suddenly aging. "Guess I hate to see my little girl march down the aisle and replace me with another man," he admitted with a wistful smile that tugged his lips upward.

Laura Lee hunched to the carpet and placed her cheek on his knee. "Judd can never replace you. I don't love you any less or him any more. It's a different kind of love. Long ago I read something about love's being like a mighty ocean." She picked up his hand and placed a kiss on the back of it as she squeezed his fingers. "The ocean washes upon many shores without loving one sandy beach more than another. Yet each cove edging the sea is unique. Love is like that, don't you think?"

Her father blinked his moist eyes. "Hr-rrmph," he said, clearing his throat. "And there is plenty of water for everyone."

Nodding, Laura Lee kissed his hand again. "You're the best dad a girl could ever have, as precious to me as water is to life."

She felt his hand caress the top of her head the way it had years ago when she was a child. Tears gathered in her eyes. Too often it was too late before a child expressed how much she loved her parent. Laura Lee wasn't going to miss this chance. She wasn't mouthing platitudes; she spoke from her heart.

"You know, Dad, Judd has many of the same qualities you have. He's kind, funny, handsome, but most important, he's my friend. That's something I've admired about your marriage. You and Mom are each other's best friend. I don't want to be like the married couples who wake up one morning and realize they don't like the person they're sleeping with nightly. You and Mom will always wake up friends. I hope I'm that lucky."

A single tear slipped down her father's cheek. He bent his forefinger and placed it under her chin. "No man could have a better daughter. You've always made me proud to call you my own." He wiped the moisture away from his cheek on the sleeve of his shirt. "Your mother says I'm going through a middle-aged crisis or something. Watching the first child permanently leave the nest is rough on the old man."

"What's the old line about not losing a daughter but gaining a son?" she said to lighten the mood.

Her father laughed. "Thank you, but I have a son. I just don't want to be shuffled into the background by my daughter. And since you mentioned my best friend, would you mind not mentioning my dropping over to your mother? She explicitly told me not to bother you with my foolishness the day before your wedding."

He rose to his feet and gave her a brief hug and a kiss on the cheek. "Just remember, Judd is a good man, but if you change your mind before you say 'I do,' I'll be there to walk you back up the aisle. Don't get some silly notion in your head about embarrassing the family. We want you to be happy."

"I'll be happy . . . once Judd and I are married and headed out of town. Did you and Mom have the myriad problems I seem to be over-whelmed by?"

"Tests your fortitude, doesn't it?" he queried with a broad smile. "Anyone who can survive what you've been through shouldn't have any problems that can't be dealt with." He chuckled, adding teasingly, "Until you have feisty children complicating your life."

"Dad, I've heard you tell everyone what a sweet child I've always been," she protested, smiling, as they walked to the door.

Playfully he swatted at her rear end. "Parents stretch the truth. How could I tell our friends who had model A plus children that my little girl gave a boy in her class a black eye for stealing a kiss out on the playground during recess?"

Laughing at the long-forgotten memory, she gave her dad an affectionate hug and then watched him amble down the sidewalk toward his car. Until now she hadn't noticed how much gray he had in his hair. His walk no longer depicted youthful, hurried strides. He waved, climbing into his dark sedan.

Getting married wasn't easy on any of them.

The phone ring brought her out of her pleasant reverie.

"Laura Lee, are you sitting down?" her mother asked, skipping the social amenities.

"What's happened?"

The thread of panic in her mother's voice was

easily heard. She could feel herself getting numb from her head to her toes. Was her mother sick, too? Had something happened to her dad? Kathy?

"I'm at the Simpsons' restaurant. Oh, my dear, I don't know how to tell you this."

"Give it to me straight, Mom."

"Everything was fine until we put the fruit-cake with the bride and groom ornament on," her mother babbled.

"The ornament broke?" Laura Lee asked, dreading her mother's response.

"Yes . . ."

"I'll bring another one over," Laura Lee replied, relieved by such a trivial mishap. "It could have been worse. The—"

"Cake collapsed!" her mother whispered before Laura Lee could complete her sentence.

"The whole thing?"

"I'm afraid so, dear. We were putting the top layer on the inverted champagne glasses, and . . . splosh, it all crumpled to the floor. Laura Lee? Laura Lee? Are you there?"

Knees sagging, no longer able to support her weight, Laura Lee did some crumpling of her own. "Oh, Mom! We can't have a proper wedding without a cake."

"It's going to be all right, dear. Judd called the bakery they do business with and arranged to have another cake delivered. He was very . . . resourceful."

"You sound perturbed, Mother. Why?"

"It's nothing for you to worry about, Laura Lee."

"Mother! What else happened?"

"He laughed. Here the cake was, hunks of it plopping onto the carpet, squashed beyond recognition . . . and he threw back his head and . . . laughed!"

"What did you expect him to do? Cry? We should be thankful he had the presence of mind to call the bakery." Laura Lee heard her mother's quick intake of breath. "I'm sorry, Mom. He shouldn't have laughed when the cake fell in. Could I speak to him?"

Laura Lee counted to ten slowly while she waited for Judd to come to the phone. Didn't she have enough on her mind today without her future husband's offending her mother? He'd have to apologize.

"Laura Lee? Guess your mother phoned about the cake falling in. You should have been here. It was like something out of a cartoon. Funnier than a pie fight."

"You laughed at my mother," Laura Lee said accusingly.

As though he hadn't heard her accusation, he chuckled, then continued. "You should have seen it. Reminded me of seeing a building dyna-mited."

"You laughed at my mother!" Laura Lee shouted. "What kind of man laughs at his future mother-in-law as his wedding cake explodes?"

"Wait a minute. I did not laugh at your mother. If you had been here and it hadn't been your precious wedding cake, you would have laughed, too. Be objective."

"Objective?" Laura Lee squawked. "Objec-tive is when it isn't happening to your mother or your cake!"

"Our cake. And I apologized to your mother for laughing at an inopportune moment." He lowered his voice. "But I do wish I had a movie of it."

"Judd Simpson, I'm not certain this wedding was meant to be."

"You're kidding!"

"I'm serious. I've never heard of anyone's wedding plans running amok like this."

"You're upset."

Stomach churning, throat clogging, she re-torted, "Brilliant deduction, Watson!"

"Calm down, Laura Lee. You can't call the wedding off because the cake fell in."

"I can!"

"Okay, but I have one question. Do you love me enough to marry me?"

51

"Of course I do. It isn't that I don't love you—"

Judd chuckled. "Great. See you at seven o'clock at the church."

"Wait a . . ." She banged the phone down. *It'd serve him right if I didn't show up,* Laura Lee thought threateningly without conviction.

With her temper boiling, she stamped over to the thermostat and flipped it back to a 55 reading. *I am not going to be mad on my wedding day.* She fumed silently. *I'm going to be quiet, serene, happy, dammit! Brides are supposed to glide down the aisle with a radiant glow on their faces. I'm going down the aisle hopping mad!*

The air conditioning clicked on, blowing cool air from a nearby vent. She raised her fists toward the ceiling and shook them at the fates, who were constantly nipping at her happiness.

"I can love you without marrying you if I want to," Laura Lee shouted illogically at the striped wallpaper.

She worked herself up into an uncontrollable redhead's fit. Bottling her inner rage hadn't prevented any misfortunes. Being sweet-tempered hadn't prevented the calamities. So why bother? Anxiety, built up over the past few days, erupted like a tornado contained in a glass jar. The lid detonated. Shards of anger shattered her self-control.

"Nobody laughs at my mother and gets away with it," she yelled as loud as she could. "Nobody! You're just lucky I'm too angry to call you back. I can call off the wedding if I really want to. I'll get even with you for the way you're treating my mother! And I—"

The phone pealed for the second time that morning. Thoroughly disgusted with Judd's cavalier treatment and certain he was calling back to apologize, she picked up the receiver. "Go to hell!" she shouted into the phone.

There was a long pause during which no one spoke. Then she heard a voice. "The congregation will be disappointed if I do. This is Reverend Jones at the church."

Laura Lee clamped her hand over her mouth. Had she really told the minister who was going to conduct her wedding service to go to hell? *Tell me I didn't do that,* she begged silently. *Maybe if I hang up, he'll think he got the wrong number.* Slowly she began lowering the receiver.

"Don't hang up, Laura Lee. I recognized your voice."

"Reverend Jones," she squeaked, "I thought it was someone else."

"No doubt," he sagely replied. "You aren't the first bride who pointed my soul in a southerly direction. Brides tend to get upset on their wedding day."

"That's putting it mildly. What's happened? Did the church burn down?"

The minister chuckled, understanding the tizzy brides usually found themselves in on the day of their wedding. "The flowers arrived. They're as beautiful as the bride-to-be. Would you like to come over to the church to make certain they are what you ordered?"

Why bother? Laura Lee thought. *The florist can deliver funeral wreaths, and I really don't care.*

"I'll be there an hour before the wedding. If you say they are beautiful, I'll take your word for it." She considered telling him about the cake's falling in and her fiancé's laughing at her mother, but decided against it. "Reverend Jones, I do apologize for answering the phone the way I did. I am a bit nervous and excited."

"That's to be expected. Everything is going to be wonderful. When a man and woman join together in holy matrimony . . ."

She felt obligated to listen to what she knew would be a portion of the lengthy sermon he had scheduled for the wedding but found her mind drifting away from what she heard. Goose bumps prickled her skin. She didn't know whether they were from the rapidly descending temperature in the room, the deflation following her blowup, or the timbre of Reverend Jones's well-modulated voice.

". . . and so what God has joined together, let no man put asunder."

"Thank you, Reverend. Talking to you has helped. I'm getting dressed at the church, as planned. Will my arrival at six be okay?"

"Certainly. I'll see you then."

"Good-bye," she said civilly, totally forgetting to apologize.

Chagrined at the results of her self-detonation, Laura Lee evaluated the situation. The emotional tornado had wildly spun, struck, then hopped and skipped out of her life. The entire trappings of the big hullabaloo could fall apart, and she would still want to marry Judd. Nothing else mattered.

Act as though this were a normal day in your life, she sternly instructed herself. *Be objective. Smile.* She forced a twisted smile to her lips. *Only crazies talk to themselves out loud. That's okay. On your wedding day you're entitled to be a little crazy.*

Organized to the hilt, Laura Lee scheduled hourly sections of time. She would pack her bags with silky lingerie, soak in a tub of cinnabar fragrance, eat a light lunch, take a short nap, allow plenty of time to apply her makeup . . . but first, she would unplug the phone! She couldn't be informed of any other disasters if the communication lines were down.

Hours later she parked her convertible in front of the church. Feeling rested and beautiful, Laura Lee removed the gown and headpiece from the back seat of the car.

Miraculously the clouds were parting, and glimmers of sunshine were peeking out. As she entered between the carved double doors of the church, she smelled the romantic fragrance of honeysuckle. As she glanced into the sanctuary, her gray eyes widened in awe. Tall candlesticks stood on each side of the minister's pulpit. At every other pew a hurricane lamp decorated with trailing vines and blossoms lent a celestial air to the church.

In an hour the overhead lights would be dimmed, the candles lit. The bridesmaids, dressed in yellow gingham covered with lacy organdy and carrying two dozen yellow roses, would enter. They would march slowly down the aisle to the melody of a traditional wedding song. Then and only then would the reality of getting married seem joyous. Until that time the entire ceremony remained fantasy.

Laura Lee dabbed the perspiration from her forehead with a Kleenex. Air conditioning? If it weren't turned on soon, the candles and the bride would melt in this heat. She draped her gown and headpiece over the back pew.

"Reverend Jones?" she called when she saw a hunched form in black praying in the front pew.

"Laura Lee! I've been trying to reach you all day. Your phone must have gone on the fritz. The air conditioning is broken, and the parts won't be here until next week. I thought maybe you would rather get dressed at home where it's cool."

Stopping in midstride, she gasped, "No air conditioning?"

"The fans will be here shortly." The Reverend Mr. Jones nervously chuckled. "When you told me to go to hell, you didn't expect to join me, did you?"

"Poetic justice?"

"Ecclesiastic joke," the minister replied. "I put a small fan in the choir room. Your mother, sister, and Lynda are already back there."

Reverend Jones waited while the bride gathered her belongings, then led the way through a small door to the side of the sanctuary. Laura Lee could hear feminine giggles from down the hallway. It was going to be tough to keep herself from breaking into hysterical laughter.

"I'll come and give you a ten-minute signal," the Reverend Mr. Jones said with a sympathetic smile. "This is an old church. Many of the first couples married here didn't have air conditioning either. Most of them are celebrating their fiftieth wedding anniversaries."

Laura Lee nodded. What difference did lack of air conditioning make? She was here to get married, not to get temporary relief from the early-summer heat. In less than an hour and a half she would be married to Judd. *Nothing else matters*, she reminded herself.

"We'll cope," she said reassuringly to the minister and swept into the choir room to resounding cries of "She's here!"

Her mother and sister hugged her shoulders fiercely.

"Hey, Mom, Kathy, you're about to strangle the star of this show," she complained, laughing at their exuberance. "Did you think I wasn't coming?"

"Everybody has been trying to call you today, but something must be wrong with your phone. I almost drove over to check you out"—her mother winked—"and give you a mother-daughter lecture."

Kathy enthusiastically jumped up and down. "Great! Do I get to listen?"

"Young lady, when you're an hour away from your own wedding, I'll talk to you about S-E-X."

"Mother, how are you going to talk about it when you spell it rather than say the word?" Laura Lee said teasingly as Lynda squeezed between the family members and gave her a swift hug.

"Actually I wrote the directions down for you." She pointed to a small gift-wrapped box and a large card lying on the hymnal shelf. "But you can't open the card until you're safely inside your honeymoon suite."

"I miss out on all the fun," Kathy said, stifling her giggle with the palm of her hand. "You guys are NF."

Mrs. Mason stepped away from Laura Lee and hugged her younger daughter. "More initials? I swear, I spend a fortune sending you to college and the only thing you've learned is a complete vocabulary of initials."

"NF means 'no fun,' " said Kathy to explain the feigned indignity. Wiggling her eyebrows à la her favorite comedian, she added, "And tonight is going to be fun, fun, fun! Huh, Laura Lee?"

"Don't be bawdy," Mrs. Mason said chastisingly. "Let's get the bride dressed!"

Amid lighthearted banter, the three women began dressing Laura Lee for the impending occasion. The ritual of something old, something new, something borrowed, something blue had them boisterously laughing. Her mother gave her a lace-edged handkerchief to tuck into the long sleeve of her gown. Lynda gave her a brand-new penny to put into her shoe. Kathy placed a racy blue garter right above her knee. And her mother lent her a treasured gift: the pearl earrings she had been given on her twentieth anniversary.

"You look like a beautiful, radiant bride," Mrs.

Mason complimented her, dabbing at her eyes with the back of her hand. "But I'm not going to cry. I've promised myself this is a happy occasion and I'm not going to cry!"

"Go ahead, Mom," Kathy said encouragingly. "What's a little PDE at a wedding?"

Lynda groaned. "What's PDE?"

Kathy answered, "Public display of emotion." She glanced at her watch. "Almost the ETA."

"Estimated time of arrival!" Lynda guessed.

"Right on," Mrs. Mason chimed in, copying one of her daughter's favorite phrases. "The organ music has begun."

A light tap on the door broke through the last-minute chatter.

"Mrs. Mason, could I speak to you for a moment?" the Reverend Mr. Jones inquired through the closed door.

As her mother slipped through the door, Laura Lee wondered what the private conference was all about. As her gray eyes widened, a terrible thought entered her head: *Judd isn't here. I'm about to be jilted at the altar!*

Not waiting for the bad news, heart thumping loudly, she swung the door open just in time to hear the minister say, "Don't tell her."

"Don't tell me what?" Laura Lee demanded.

Distressed looks passed between the minister and her mother.

"Don't tell me what?" Laura Lee's voice lowered to a deathly hush. "Judd isn't coming, is he?"

"Judd is here. It's his parents who are late," the minister said with a weak smile.

"His parents aren't coming to the wedding of their only son?" Laura Lee said with a relieved giggle.

Mrs. Mason patted her shoulders comfortingly. "They'll be here. There was a tractor-trailer accident on the highway, and the Simpsons' car was detained. Let's go back into the choir room and wait. It's cooler in there."

The bride couldn't help wondering if the disapproving parents had planned the blockage of the highway. *No*, she silently rebuked herself. *They might have preferred Judd to marry a social debutante, but surely they wouldn't* . . .

"Why don't we have the girls put their hats on and have the photographer take some pictures?" Mrs. Mason suggested, turning toward the door, determined to keep her daughter's spirits up.

Dazed, Laura Lee allowed herself to be posed in various positions. The photographer's lights increased the temperature ten degrees. The handkerchief her mother had given her was soaking wet and blotched with makeup. Was it possible for a bride to go into shock after suffering a heat stroke? she wondered when the perspiration began dripping off the tip of her nose.

The bouquet of white rosebuds intermingled with the yellow orchids the florist brought were drooping. Head bowed, Laura Lee sympathized. Too many minidisasters were beginning to take their toll. She could picture herself stretched out on the metal folding chairs, growing older and older while they waited for Judd's parents.

"They're here!" the Reverend Mr. Jones announced gleefully. "Come on, Mrs. Mason, girls. We have a wedding to attend!"

CHAPTER FOUR

An attack of nerves unlike any Laura Lee had ever experienced paralyzed her. The strip of brass separating the tiled foyer from the carpeted aisle could have marked the brink of the world's deepest chasm.

Candlelight lit the sanctuary with a golden glow. Her father watched for the predetermined signal from the front of the church. As though she were viewing the entire scene through tunnel vision, she saw only Judd.

Standing erect, his summer white tuxedo contrasting with the dark tones of his skin and hair, his capable hands clasped together below his waist, he waited. As Kathy stepped out of the aisle, moving to her position at the altar, the grin on Judd's handsome face widened, displaying even rows of white teeth. He seemed to take a step forward, toward her.

Laura Lee wasn't aware of how pale her skin had become. Enveloped in a cloud of filmy lace, she appeared almost unreal in her beauty. A smile trembled on her lips when her father took her hand and placed it in the crook of his elbow. Palms sweating, knees weak, she crossed the threshold in perfect time to the music. Her gray eyes locked with Judd's glowing dark eyes as she was propelled forward.

It was as though they were alone in the church. Step by measured step Laura Lee closed the gap between them. At the end of the aisle her father brushed a kiss on her pale cheek and removed her tight hold from his arm.

With his entire face smiling, Judd took the limp, damp hand extended toward him. All her senses focused on Judd. She could feel the strength of his arm, could smell the clean, woodsy fragrance of his aftershave, could hear the even pace of his breathing. The rapid beating of her heart slowed to match his. Her breathing slackened its pace. Her eyes never leaving his, she silently communicated her love.

They were united as one before the minister spoke the first word.

When Laura Lee slid into her car on the passenger seat, she couldn't for the world have described the wedding reception. She must have greeted their guests, must have swallowed the wedding cake Judd poked into her mouth, must have thrown the garter to the men and the bridal bouquet to the unmarried women. But it was all a rosy haze.

"Ready to investigate lovely white ceilings?" Judd asked in a gravelly tone.

Words stuck in Laura Lee's throat.

"We are!" Vanessa chimed in from the back seat. Her bleached blond head leaned forward into the front seat between Judd and Laura Lee. "Got plenty of gas?"

"Get back here, Mrs. McDougal," Mac said as he hauled his bride backward. "We're going to indulge in some heavy necking while our chauffeur drives us to our honeymoon retreat."

"Why don't you put your head on my shoulder?" Judd suggested to Laura Lee. "You look exhausted."

As her head touched the fabric of his short-sleeve summer shirt, she heard Vanessa say, "The bedraggled bride. Poor dear. Quit it, Mac. I don't want to neck; I want to talk!"

Closing her eyes and her ears, Laura Lee didn't hear anything else. She was tired, too tired to think of a snappy comeback. The drive to the Ozarks would take three hours. Laura Lee sealed her lips. Once they had left Vanessa and Mac in a hotel room, then her own honeymoon would begin.

Judd kissed the top of his wife's head. *My wife,* he mused, heading toward the highway. *Someone of my very own to share my life with.* The thought pleased him. He shifted his arm to hold his wife closer.

A long tendril of copper-colored hair had slipped loose from her upswept hair. The moonlight shining through the front window danced through the golden highlights. Idly his fingers twined the errant lock between them.

Vanessa, chirping incessantly in the back seat, was Mac's problem.

Three vertical lines marred the space between Judd's brows. His bride had been so untypically quiet since the wedding. When the Reverend Mr. Jones asked if she would take Judd Simpson to be her lawfully wedded husband, she had replied softly, "I beg your pardon?"

When he lifted her hand to put the diamond wedding band on her fourth finger, it was shaking so badly he felt as though he were trying to put a ring on a fluttering bird. Her silver eyes never left his face. It was as though she were drawing on his stamina to sustain herself through the ceremony.

Tenderly he caressed her cheek. *Do elaborate weddings cause a form of shellshock? Or battle fatigue?* he wondered. He smiled wryly when he glanced into the rearview mirror and saw Mac capture Vanessa's moving lips. He realized his first night of marriage would be spent cuddling his new bride. Judd didn't mind. The wedding and the reception had been an ordeal he would refuse to participate in again.

Judd chuckled. Laura Lee smiled in her deep sleep and burrowed more closely under the shelter of his arm. She would have a fit if she found out what had taken place between their fathers toward the end of the reception. His arm protectively snuggled her closer. He'd keep any unpleasantness away from his wife. *That's what husbands are for, isn't it?* he rationalized.

Humming along with the easy listening music on the car stereo, Judd stroked Laura Lee soothingly. He looked forward to the seven days' uninterrupted vacation. Do a little swimming, a little loving, a little water skiing, a little loving, maybe some fishing, definitely more loving! Happy at the prospect, he mentally drew a line through swimming, skiing, and fishing.

Although the guests at the wedding would never testify to Laura Lee's spontaneous laughter, her quick wit, her sharp tongue, he knew them well. Individuality set her apart from other women. No man, himself included, would ever dominate his headstrong wife. She had a will of her own and didn't hesitate to express it.

Again Judd quietly laughed. But he had found the means of reducing reluctance to acquiescence. Laura Lee might dig her heels in as he dragged her across the plush carpet of the bedroom, but once they were in bed, she was passionate putty in his experienced hands.

When she teased him about getting his way via sex, they both knew there was a golden thread of truth in the humor. Judd hoped it would never change. With Laura Lee he felt ten feet tall, strong as a giant, and virile as the star of a porno flick.

His mobile face frowned. *But I'll have to get her out of this quiet passivity,* he thought. *I'd rather hear her screaming bloody murder than watch her meekly submissive.* What was he worried about? Laura Lee would recover her spunkiness after a good night's sleep.

Laura Lee's subconscious had carefully saved the wedding ceremony and reception for her to view in the privacy of her sleep. Without the frightening emotions of dread and fear, an instant replay colored her exhausted sleep.

One by one she greeted friends and acquaintances in the reception line. Merrily each of them kissed her cheek or shook her hand and wished happiness. They congratulated the beaming groom on his selection of a mate. Judd attentively stayed by her side.

Champagne poured freely. An ice carving of a swan spouted punch for those who didn't imbibe the wine. The long buffet table, decorated with flowers and silver, held a delightful array of culinary delights that would tempt the most jaded palate. In the back of the dining room, a large, creamy wedding cake dominated another table. Although her parents would have preferred a small sit-down dinner at the swim club they belonged to, they appeared content.

The photographer moved about, snapping pictures. The dream she was having would fade, but the picture album would be cherished. A camera's eye would catch wonderful moments she had missed.

Dear, wonderful Judd saved the top layer, the iced fruitcake, from the cake her mother's friend had baked. It was his way of apologizing to her mother for laughing at the wrong time. Wrapped in foil, frozen, he showed Mrs. Mason the cake and told her they would celebrate their first wedding anniversary by eating a slice.

Laura Lee could almost taste the sugary confection Judd placed in her mouth after they had jointly sliced the first piece to share. She could feel the softened icing on her fingertips as she gingerly held the remainder of the slice up to his lips. Their arms linked, she drained the wine from his glass and he drank the champagne from hers.

Her memories intact, Laura Lee felt at peace.

"Sweetheart." She heard her husband's voice near her ear. "We're at Tan-Tar-A."

"Mmmmm," she groggily responded. If they could drive a bit farther, perhaps she would remember who had caught the garter and the flowers.

"Well, I guess Laura Lee will be okay in the car while we check in."

"I'll go with you," Vanessa volunteered. "Mac is sound asleep too."

The alarm ringing in the back of Laura Lee's mind wasn't loud enough to awaken her completely. Eyes closed, head uncomfortably leaning against the headrest, she willed her subconscious to finish the dream. *Who caught the flowers?* she silently asked.

Bridal bouquet in hand, she remembered turning her back to the group of laughing single women after mentally marking where her friend Lynda stood. Why had she moved to the back of the group? It would take a mighty heave to guarantee that Lynda caught them. Knees dipping, arms swinging down, Laura Lee pitched them as hard as she could over her shoulder. Oh, no! Oh, no! Getting an instant replay, she saw the flowers arch, then whack into the ceiling not three feet from her heels. Kathy grabbed them.

Laura Lee groaned in her sleep. *Mom and Dad are going to kill me if she gets married before she graduates!*

"Wake up, love," Judd said as he climbed back into the car and slammed the door. "Mac, didn't you make reservations?"

"Huh?" Mac drowsily questioned from the back seat.

"Didn't you make reservations for tonight?" Vanessa nearly shouted into her husband's ear.

"My secretary made reservations for the fifth of June through the eleventh," Mac stated emphatically.

"Today is the fourth, and there aren't any rooms available for tonight."

"What time is it?" Laura Lee asked Judd.

"After one. We'll have a hell of a time finding a place."

The long nap had restored Laura Lee's vitality. The weary bride was replaced by the fun-loving woman she had been before the wedding disasters. Scooting over to his side, she whispered, "Trade one lovely white ceiling in for nature's star-studded ceiling."

Judd hugged her. Nibbling on her ear, he whispered playfully, "We've never made love in a car."

"Isn't it going to be slightly crowded with four in the back seat?" she asked teasingly.

"Quit telling secrets," Vanessa interrupted. "Dumb butt screwed up."

"Are you referring to me or my secretary?" Mac said grumpily.

"You! I'm not sleeping in the back seat of a car on my honeymoon," she trilled in a shrill voice.

Mac's temper flared. "You never minded the

back seat of my car. Shut up. Sit back and cool off. This isn't the only resort in the Ozarks. Judd, let's try the other big resorts first. Then we'll try the small ones. The bed may not be king-size, but we'll find something."

And they did. At three in the morning they pulled up in front of a two-bedroom cabin twenty miles past the resort area. The lake was a good five miles away from their lodging.

Laura Lee surprised herself. The more Vanessa griped, moaned, and groaned, the better she felt. Her tinkling laughter mingled and contrasted with the high-pitched tones behind her. Poor Mac had been called everything but husband.

Joining in her laughter, Judd opened the car door on her side and lifted her out.

"This may not be the plush resort I'd planned on, but I'm going to make up for it by carrying you across the threshold." Judd planted a smacking loud kiss on her lips, and in high spirits, he tossed Laura Lee into the air several times.

Laura Lee squealed joyfully. The traditional wedding had been an ordeal, but the honeymoon would make up for it by being glorious.

"Aren't you going to carry me in?" Vanessa demanded.

"You're an old married lady of two days. Your feet work fine. Use the rubber sole express," Mac told her.

Over Judd's shoulder Laura Lee watched Mac get out of the car and open the trunk. Listening to Vanessa, she learned the meaning of "cussing a blue streak." Giggling, Laura Lee peppered her husband's neck with sharp, tingling kisses.

"Which room?" Judd asked as he lowered her to her feet in the sitting area of the cabin.

"Uh-oh." When Laura Lee looked into the open bedroom doors, she saw a common wall between the two brass beds. She walked into the room on the right and tapped the paper-thin wall. "Something tells me the bed squeaks."

Judd immediately tested the double bed out by falling backward onto it. He knew he'd made a mistake when he heard a loud, groaning noise of protest. Then the foot of the bed sank to the floor. By the time he managed to recover his balance he heard his bride and Mac laughing uproariously in the doorway.

"Glad you chose that one, ol' buddy," Mac said, ribbing him. "We'll take the other bedroom."

Clutching her sides in laughter at the ridiculous picture Judd had made as his arms flailed when the end of the bed tilted, Laura Lee missed the malicious smirk on Vanessa's face.

"Carry the bags in while I fix the bed." Judd chuckled as he rolled to the hardwood planked floor.

"Do I look like a bellhop?" Laura said teasingly, refusing to budge an inch.

Judd jackknifed to his feet and swooped her into his arms. "Forget the bags, wife. We don't need bedclothes."

"Oh, yes, we do. I bought a nightgown specially for my wedding night, and I'm going to wear it," Laura Lee answered in a cheery tone.

"Okay. Okay." Judd bent over and glanced at his reflection in the old-fashioned mirror. "Slave, tote those bags."

He moved outside the bedroom door and brought them in, pretending they weighed a ton. "That's it," he said lightly. "Now you'll have to fix the bed."

When closing the door behind Judd, Laura Lee could hear the bickering still taking place through the pine-paneled wall. On tiptoe she crossed the room. Her slender arms wound around her husband's neck.

"Feel adventuresome?" A wicked light entered her gray eyes as she asked the question.

Loud sobbing could be heard from next door.

"More and more. Any suggestions?" Judd answered. His face lit up at the prospect of Laura Lee's being her spunky self once more.

"With the next crescendo from"—her auburn hair tangled in his hands as she tilted it to the left—"the charming bride next door, let's sneak out of the cabin, take a blanket, and . . . ?"

74

Purposely Laura Lee let her voice lilt upward. The idea of making love in the back seat of the car intrigued Judd. A marriage certificate certainly lowered his bride's level of inhibition, he thought, pleased with the plan forming in his mind.

"Back Seat Bride?" he said.

"Or Splendor in the Grass," Laura Lee quipped, snuggling closer.

The caterwauling next door increased in volume. Mac could be heard shouting, "Vanessa, you're impossible. You don't hear Laura Lee screaming, do you?"

"That insipid broad doesn't have any emotions. She is probably snoring in Judd's ear."

"I'd like to catch a few *Z's* myself. Get out of the middle of the bed," Mac instructed tiredly.

"You're not sleeping with *me!* No caviar? No champagne? No action!"

"I think that's our exit line," Judd whispered as he grabbed the blankets off the bed and took Laura Lee's hand.

Together the crept out of the room. The floorboards squeaked, but with the fighting and fussing going on in the other room, neither Judd nor Laura Lee bothered to suffocate their hushed laughter with their palms.

"My nightgown!" Laura Lee pulled her hand away and ran back into the room.

"I'll be out on the porch," Judd whispered.

Seconds later Laura Lee, filmy nightgown in hand, tiptoed out the front door.

"The Battle of the Bed still ensuing?" he asked.

"Shhhh. Let's get out of here. Mac is going to sleep in the car. Vanessa said she would rather . . ." Laura Lee could feel a red stain sweeping over her high cheekbones.

His eyes adjusted to the meager light coming through the tall trees surrounding the cabin, Judd took her by the elbow and directed her toward a path on the left side of the cabin. "Don't stop now. How is Vanessa planning to spend the night?"

"Just never you mind, Judd Simpson. Do you know where this path goes?" she asked, hoping to change the direction of the conversation.

"Nope, but I have high hopes. Now answer the question."

"What question?" Laura Lee asked with pseudoinnocence.

"How is Vanessa going to spent the night once Mac has vacated the premises?"

"Gosh! I've forgotten. Shall I go back and ask?" she said jokingly.

"Laura Lee Simpson," Judd growled in a threatening voice as he spun around and grabbed her by the waist.

"I like the sound of that. Laura"—she threaded her hands through his dark mane of hair—"Lee"—raising one leg, she rubbed sensually against his outer thigh—"Simpson." His predictable reaction wiped from her mind any doubt as to how they were going to spend the night.

"Wife," Judd intoned with tenderness.

Their kiss began with sweetness, ended with starved passion. Judd cupped his hands behind her upper thighs and silently directed them to rest around his hips. He supported their combined, entwined bodies with ease.

Once, twice, he started to break away from the kiss and find a comfortable place for them to spread the blanket he had dropped, but he couldn't find the strength.

He inhaled her breath as though pure country air wouldn't sustain him. His mouth twisted over soft lips as his probing tongue fought for supremacy. Consummating the marriage was uppermost in his thoughts. Yet he curbed the desire to drop to the blanket, strip her summer dress off her body, and make her officially his.

"Laura Lee," he gasped, loosening his tight hold on her upper thighs. "Making love outside agrees with you. You're a wild woman tonight."

Surprised at her own wantonness, she laughed nervously. Had he been offended by her forthrightness? His legs trembled; the flesh beneath her hand burned. No. Judd wasn't repulsed. Not in the least.

"Care to take a stroll down the wild side of my nature?" she asked, rocking her elevated torso against him as she tightened the muscles in her buttocks.

"Honey, what makes me think I'm in for the best night of my lust-filled life?"

"This?" she asked. The tip of her tongue circled the shell of his ear as she blew a husky breath of air at the same time.

Judd couldn't speak; he groaned; he tightened the viselike clamp on her posterior.

"Or this?"

She shimmied the tips of her diamond-hard breasts against the front of his shirt. Her lips strung moist kisses along his chiseled jawline.

Judd knew he could not take much more provocative teasing. "Can you keep that train of thought long enough for us to travel a bit farther down the path?"

Unwrapping her legs, Laura Lee leaned against him long enough to recover her balance. Gracefully she stooped and picked up the blanket and gown.

"Lead the way, husband. I'll follow."

"For a change," Judd said teasingly. He yelped when she smacked his rear end.

"You're courting disaster with your tongue," Laura Lee said jokingly.

"We'll see," he replied with a chuckle.

Minutes later they stepped into a small open

clearing. Wordlessly each of them took a corner of the blanket and spread it on the ground.

"Where's the dressing room?" Laura asked, trying to keep a serious tone.

Judd looked around. "That way, m'lady." He pointed back toward the path they had just left.

Nodding, smiling, waving her nightgown, Laura Lee departed. Once she was hidden from view, she quickly dispensed with her clothing. Happy, she hummed a nonsensical tune, then softly sang her own lyrics:

"Naked in the woods beneath the moon,/Oh, honey, what a honeymoon!"

She laughed at her own naughtiness.

"Do I hear you singing?" Judd queried in disbelief.

"Uh-huh. I always sing when I'm happy," she answered.

"You have ten seconds, Mrs. Simpson. I have to get undressed, too," he complained mischievously.

Laura Lee slipped into her diaphanous white gown and sang a whisper louder: "Impatient lover waiting,/His fever not abating." She paused, trying to find the right words to conclude the ditty.

Judd quietly approached. Picking up her tune, he sang in a baritone voice: "His wife slowly appears,/She'll be his life, his love . . . for years."

Raising her head, listening to his husky composition, Laura Lee gazed at his lithe, athletic naked body. He raised his hand, silently beckoning her back to their wedding bed.

A breeze carried her quietly spoken vow. "I love you, Judd Simpson, eternally."

Judd grinned in a way that twisted her heart. Fingertips touching, they crossed back to the blanket. Together, harmoniously, they sank to the ground and fell into each other's arms.

"How could I date you, be engaged to you, and discover on my wedding night I've married a composer?" Judd asked. One hand on each side of her face, he leaned close and studied her as though he had made a fantastic discovery.

"You thought you had uncovered all my womanly secrets?"

She traced the outline of his collarbone with her fingers. Lightly she placed one finger on the vein throbbing steadily in his neck.

"Are you suggesting there are other secrets you've been hiding? Perhaps the wild lady I met back on the path?" he asked. "Have you been holding back on me?"

Laura Lee seductively lowered one eyelid. "Do you have a preference for wild, naked forest nymphs?"

A shaft of fire scorched up his spine as her fingers magically massaged the back of his neck. Judd caught the satin straps of her nightgown and lowered them. The sheer, cobweblike lace clung to the swell of her breasts. Slowly he inched the protective covering to her waist.

"I prefer you"—he caressed each breast with his fingers and palms—"to any woman. I married you."

Laura Lee knew those words were the highest compliment a woman could receive. Impatient to feel his skin against her own, she raised her hips and removed the billowing gown. The smile on her lover's face told her she had done the right thing. His dark eyes smoldered in the moonlight as they memorized each peak, each valley, each change of color and texture.

"You're sleek," she said praisingly. "Your body is magnificent."

She watched his eyebrow peak in surprise. They had conducted their lovemaking in silence previously. Tonight she wanted to tell him all the things she had thought.

Her hand raised to caress first the short hairs at the nape of his neck and then the fine hairs curling on his massive chest. Lastly, they followed the natural path below his waist.

He jolted as though a current of electricity had coursed through each place she touched.

"I love the feel of your skin and the manly hair covering it."

Her toes raked up the back of his calves to the sensitive area behind his knees. Using her fingernails, she lightly scored a path through the dark mat on his chest. She circled one flat male nipple, then the other. They both became erect under her ministrations.

His breath quickened. Judd draped one leg over her upper thighs, letting her see the effect of her touch, her praise. His hands began brushing strokes from her shoulder to her hip.

"You make my heart strum inside my chest, strum with a song no one but you can hear."

She captured his hand and put the palm over her heart. "I bite my tongue to keep from shouting your name when you're inside me."

"Call my name. Let the creatures of the forest hear you," Judd whispered. "I want you, Laura Lee, my wife, my love."

Beneath a blanket of star-studded darkness, she ignited a flame that could be seen from the heavens. She no longer held her tongue idle. Anything she couldn't say she expressed with her silvery eyes.

His name became a soulful mixture of rhythm and blues. The tempo of their lovemaking pounded in each of their hearts, quickening as they climbed to the heights of passion. Neither could control the burst of desire or the rapture humming inside them after they had catapulted over the peak.

"Judd. Judd."

As he staked his marital claim, she made a

golden discovery of her own: Their marriage would be like a gold mine. Every time they physically united a trace of pure gold would be brought to the surface for each of them to cherish.

The moon's light made the diamond on her wedding band sparkle. Silently she tucked the memory among those of the wedding. Contentedly she sighed. *Golden wedding, golden anniversary, years of loving and being loved* were her last thoughts as Judd pulled the spare blanket over both of them.

At dawn she awakened, feeling Judd's tongue painting a message from her belly to the shadow between her breasts. She smiled, knowing Judd invariably awakened with a sunny disposition. When his tongue tickled a word over her ribs, she huskily laughed.

"Are you taking lesson in Braille?" she asked lightheartedly.

"Giving them," he replied huskily.

"Hmmm. I'm a slow learner. You'll have to tell me what the message says."

"Disaster!"

"What?" Laura Lee pushed his head away from her stomach.

Judd laughed and gave her a swift kiss. "Last night you said my tongue was courting disaster. I wrote 'disaster' in capital letters across the front of your sexy body. Now I won't mind courting it!"

Hugging him close, Laura Lee joined in his laughter.

As she cuddled against her husband, the early summer's sunrays painted the sky orange, then red, before the fiery ball slowly began its ascent to a clear blue zenith. White ceilings and the comfort of a feather bed couldn't compete with nature's daily display.

"How do you think Mac and Vanessa are getting along?" Judd lazily asked.

Laura Lee heard an element of smugness in his voice. Was he comparing the bickering and squabbling with the bliss they had shared? A cat-that-ate-the-cream smile drew her lips upward. "Who knows?" *Or cares,* she silently added.

"By the way, you forgot to answer my question last night. What did Vanessa say she'd rather do?"

"I've forgotten. Must have been unimportant."

"Secrets? Already?" Judd asked teasingly. "I thought old married couples shared everything."

"Didn't we?"

"You're dodging the question . . . wife." Judd stressed the final word in the sentence. "Come on. 'Fess up, or I'll tickle the information out of you."

After flipping the blanket back, Laura Lee quickly jumped to her feet and called over her shoulder, "You'll have to catch me first!"

"Aha! The wood nymph flees her exhausted lover!" Judd was on his feet and in laughing pursuit within seconds.

Running and giggling are compatible, Laura Lee thought as she circled to the opposite edge of the clearing. She had no intention of telling Judd that Vanessa said she would rather sleep in a chair in the room next door and watch Judd than share a bed with her husband. A blend of green-eyed jealousy mixed with pity for Mac kept her lips sealed.

"Gotcha!" Judd crowed as he lunged.

Laura Lee feinted to the left and ran to the right. Judd grabbed thin air. Off-balance, he toppled to the dewy grass.

"I'll make you pay for that, Mrs. Simpson," he said with faked ominousness. "Five minutes of my fingers running up and down the soles of your feet!"

She darted back toward the blankets. "You've got grass stains on your knees," she said, laughing. Collapsing onto the ground, she wrapped her naked body tightly in the blanket.

Judd slowed his pace and pretended to be stalking his boisterous prey. His Vincent Price type of laughter sent shivers down Laura Lee's spine. She ducked her head beneath the covers.

"Well, well. Look what I found." Vanessa's high-pitched voice filled with the pleasure of catching Judd naked. "Lost your bride?"

Under the covers, Laura Lee groaned aloud. This wasn't the way she had intended to start the morning. But she thanked her lucky stars for being completely covered with the blanket.

"Give me the blanket." Judd issued the curt demand as he began tugging at the corner. Head raised, he shouted, "Go find your own husband."

"No way, José. I find the morning air . . . refreshing," Vanessa replied, advancing farther into the clearing.

Judd had never been embarrassed by nudity, but his viewpoint had changed. Now he wanted to save Laura Lee from any embarrassment. He couldn't jerk the blanket off his wife to cover his own nakedness and reveal her state of undress. Yet he wasn't about to let Vanessa ogle him all the way back to the cabin.

"Share and share alike," Judd muttered.

He loosened the grip Laura Lee had on the edge of the blanket and whispered, "I'm getting eaten alive out here, woman. And I don't mean by mosquitoes!"

Laura Lee instantly released her hold. Once he was beside her, she said in a low voice she hoped Vanessa couldn't hear, "I'm going to move to the edge of the bottom blanket. You wrap it around yourself, and I'll wrap the top one around myself. Ready?"

Grunting his positive response, Judd bunched the navy blue blanket around his hips. "If you have any sense of common decency, you'll be out of here, pronto!" he shouted at Vanessa. His plans for the morning didn't include an audience!

Laughing shrilly with excitement, Vanessa replied, "Sweetie, decent is boring; indecent is fun."

"Poor Mac," Laura Lee muttered quietly. "They haven't been married a week, and she has kicked him out of the honeymoon bed and is chasing his best friend."

"You don't think I'm going to tell him, do you? Mac's pride would never recover," Judd whispered. "I think Vanessa is vividly answering the question I was going to torture out of you."

"Are you covered?" Laura Lee asked.

"Yeah. I'll stand up and block the view. You wrap the top one around yourself Indian style."

Moments later Laura Lee stood behind Judd and draped the blanket over her shoulders.

"What's that scrap of material over there?" Vanessa maliciously asked. "Goodness! Mrs. Goody Two-shoes spent the night rolling in the grass!"

Laura Lee could feel the hot blood of anger bubbling upward, flushing her cheeks with banners of red. She bit her tongue. *Oh, how Vanessa would love it if I played the game by her rules,* she silently grumbled. *As she so aptly put it, "No way, José!" She'll dig her own grave . . . with her mouth.*

Pivoting, Laura Lee pasted a broad, happy smile on her face. "Good morning, Vanessa."

An expresson of shock on Judd's face, he stared at his bride. She should be verbally ripping Vanessa to pieces. *Doesn't she care if Mac's wife is trying to put the make on me?* His lips tightly compressed. "Let's get back to the cabin," he ground out for both their benefits.

"Lead the way, oh, great chief." Vanessa stepped to the side of the path and imitated a courtly bow.

Barefoot, Judd jammed his feet forward with what he wished were earthshaking strides. Not only was his wife not jealous, but her first thought was of "poor Mac." *And here I thought she didn't want them along on our honeymoon because it would destroy our privacy. Come to find out, she's probably had a secret longing to mother-hen Mac.*

Vanessa stepped behind Judd in front of Laura Lee. She cast a smirk over her shoulder at Laura Lee that plainly said, "I want your man . . . and I'll get him."

CHAPTER FIVE

Vanessa didn't know how close she had come to meeting her Maker. Flirting with Judd and making suggestive comments were one thing, but the underlying challenge she issued on the path back to the cabin was something else. Mentally Laura Lee yanked tufts of stringy bleached blond hair from Vanessa's head. Her designer shirt and slacks were torn to shreds. Long claw marks around the jugular vein told the imaginary story of her demise.

But to all outward appearances the three of them were companionably strolling back to the cabin. Mac, who was sitting on the porch in a cane-backed chair, didn't notice any tension. Vanessa was oblivious to anything other than herself. Judd pretended to be the guardian of two fragile females. And Laura Lee smiled at the thoughts of just vengeance.

"Hi, guys. Out for a morning hike?" Mac asked with a wide grin.

"I found them romping in the fields," Vanessa answered demurely.

Judd climbed the steps and leaned against the banister. "How about packing up and heading toward the resort?"

"Great," Mac said enthusiastically. "Once we drop off our bags, we can rent a boat and do some fishing and water skiing."

Gritting her teeth to keep her smile intact, Laura Lee didn't comment. Their bags were packed except for her nightgown. The moment they arrived at their planned destination she was going to do everything in her power to keep Judd hotel-bound. Wouldn't he rather take up where Vanessa had rudely interrupted than get involved with water sports? What about those lovely white ceilings? So far she hadn't seen the first one.

Judd was mystified by his wife. Why wasn't she protecting what legally was hers? She looked like a prim, grinning idiot as she calmly marched past him and into the cabin. Hadn't she noticed that Vanessa had followed him so closely up the trail he could feel the heat of her breath on the back of his neck? Couldn't she stop on the porch long enough to observe the come-and-get-it looks Vanessa furtively cast beneath her false eyelashes? Dammit! Didn't Laura Lee care enough to retaliate? *We haven't been married twenty-four hours, and she's taking me for granted!*

"How about skiing this afternoon and fishing this evening?" Judd asked without consulting Laura Lee.

When Laura Lee heard him, she could have screamed with fury. Weren't they supposed to ride to the lake together and then go their separate ways? Why hadn't Judd told them to kiss off until next Saturday? After wadding up her nightgown into a small ball, she threw it into the suitcase.

"And mattress polo tonight?" Mac leeringly suggested. "With champagne, caviar, soft music, and flower petals strewn on the bed."

Vanessa's squeaky laughter cut right through to Laura Lee's bones. She jerked on her scanty underwear and matching blue shorts and shirt as she realized she had mistakenly given Vanessa the whip hand by revealing she had little interest in skiing or fishing. No doubt Vanessa excelled at both.

The thought of putting a perfectly innocent, squirming worm on a hook repelled Laura Lee. And wasn't water skiing man's version of walking on water? With the vengeful thoughts she had been having, a bolt of lightning would probably strike the second she popped out of the water. *Well, Mrs. Simpson,* she advised herself, *don't let the rest of them know. Hide behind a smile. Give them a dose of Mason charm and grace.*

As she started to close the suitcase, she saw the envelope and small gift-wrapped package her mother had brought to the church. Closing her ears to the banter taking place in the other room, she sat down on the edge of the bed and opened the gift. Nestled in a bed of cotton lay a gold charm bracelet with a round charm engraved with a miniature replica of their wedding invitation. As a child she remembered being fascinated by a similar bracelet her mother wore on special occasions. Only her mother's had row after row of anniversary charms. *A special treasure from a special person,* Laura Lee thought.

She opened the envelope and saw a handmade card. On the outside her mother had printed: "Instructions for your wedding night." Laura Lee opened the card and laughed aloud at the message: DON'T POINT AND DON'T GIGGLE!

Returning to the sitting area in a better frame of mind, Laura Lee gave each of them a see-my-back-molars smile. "I'm ready."

"I've paid for the cabin. Let's load up and get out of here," Mac informed everyone as he picked up their suitcase.

"I love Judd's casual wear," Vanessa cooed. She swayed her hips in an exaggerated motion as she etched a visual line across his hips. "But long skirts are slightly outdated."

Her breathy laugh had the effect of claws on chalkboard for Laura Lee.

"I'll slip into something more comfortable," Judd said jokingly. "Care to pick something out of the suitcase for me?"

He addressed his question to his wife, but Vanessa answered, "I'm better at *out of* rather than *into*." She turned and waggled her index finger in Laura Lee's face. "He's starting the training period. Unless you want to go through life picking out his clothes and laying them out for him, you'd better refuse. Better to be a trainer than a trainee!"

Mac laughed uncomfortably. "Laura Lee stays in here. If the two of you see that mattress . . ." His voice trailed off suggestively.

Judd quickly slipped on a pair of pants and a T-shirt.

Twenty miles later, after registering, the two couples entered the three-story chalet that was the original building in the resort. Laura Lee, impressed by the lavish appointments in the McDougal suite, was anxious to see their accommodations on the next floor. Vanessa had oooohed and aaaahed over Mac's and her lake view, the wide-screen color TV, the huge satin-covered bed. And rightly so. It was a beautiful honeymoon suite.

Judd opened the door. Instead of a wide-screen TV, Laura Lee saw a portable black-and-white set. The twin beds were covered with serviceable plaid bedspreads. And the view? She walked to the sliding balcony doors. Unlocking the glass door, she tried to open it but couldn't. Inwardly sighing, she saw why. Evidently every pigeon in the Ozarks roosted on their balcony. The visible proof of their occupancy had gotten on the track of the sliding door, prohibiting anyone access to the balcony.

"It doesn't compare with the bridal suite, does it?" Judd commented. He tried to push the beds together but couldn't. A common headboard secured the permanent separation of them. He appreciated the brave front Laura Lee adopted. But he felt like placing a long-distance call to Mac's secretary to fire her. "Two in a single bed should be cozy," he said with false enthusiasm.

Laughing at the discrepancy between the two rooms, Laura Lee opened her arms and walked toward Judd. "The ceiling is the right color," she said temptingly.

Judd groaned. "Mac and Vanessa are coming up as soon as they slip into their swimsuits."

"Don't you think since they're on their honeymoon and didn't sleep together last night that once they get undressed, it might take them awhile?"

She unbuttoned the first three buttons of her

blouse. Her gray eyes gave him a meaningful, seductive look as she raked her hand through her windblown auburn hair.

"Sounds logical to me," Judd replied, his dark eyes warming. "Why don't I call down to make certain we aren't interrupted?"

Before he had managed to put the phone to his ear, he heard three sharp raps at the door. He banged the phone down, swung his legs over the bed to the floor, reached over, and swung the door open.

"You left your bride's wedding gifts in the trunk. I brought them up to you." Mac grinned broadly as he brushed past Judd and stepped into the room.

"We aren't ready yet," Judd gritted out.

"Vanessa isn't either. But my modest bride shooed me out of the room while she changes clothes. I figured by the time I retrieved Laura Lee's gift, you'd be ready to go."

"We were just getting ready," Judd said, disgusted by Mac's intrusion.

Mac handed Laura Lee the six-foot by three-inch package, keeping the other gaily wrapped package under his arm. "I helped Judd pick it out. You're going to love it."

"Thanks," Laura Lee muttered ungraciously. She didn't want to open the special wedding gift Judd had bought for her in front of Judd's ex-roommate.

"So open it." Mac encouraged her with an engaging, boyish smile.

As she stripped off the paper, letting it fall to the floor, and was wishing Mac hadn't arrived, her mouth dropped in surprise. *A rod and reel? My wedding gift is a fishing rod and reel?*

"Isn't it a beauty? Graphite. Judd wanted to get you a dumb piece of jewelry, but I talked him into getting you something practical. You're an accountant. You know accountants are a practical breed, aren't they?" Mac said teasingly. "Besides, this is romantic. This little baby is like a new bride: unused and fragile. Every time you go fishing over the years you'll remember your honeymoon."

What wonderful compliment can I give about a fishing pole I don't want? Laura Lee thought. "It's beautiful" didn't seem apropos. Neither did "Oh! It's something I've always wanted." Judd and Mac both were silently waiting for a response.

Glancing at the reel, she quipped, "Oh, look. It has thread already on it."

Mac looked at Judd aghast, then doubled up as he hooted with laughter. "Thread! Her reel is threaded!" Mac pounded his thighs with one open palm, which made a loud, slapping noise similar to applause.

Suppressing a smile, Judd hugged his wife.

"Monofilament, dear." He corrected her. "No one can accuse you of being a fishwife, right?"

"I've never gone fishing," she inanely explained. She kissed his cheek. "Thank you."

Judd took the other gift out from under Mac's arm. "Something to go with it."

"Terrific," Laura Lee muttered, mustering up some false enthusiasm. *No doubt this is a tackle box,* she guessed when she felt a handle through the paper. Silently she spun through her repertoire of compliments. "A tackle box," she exclaimed. "Now I have everything!"

"Not quite. Open it," Judd instructed.

She unhooked the latches, expecting the box to be filled with live worms. Instead, in neat little trays, was an array of brightly colored artificial lures. "No worms?" she asked teasingly.

"Purple ones," Mac answered, reaching down into the bottom and pulling out a strip of cardboard with rubbery worms attached.

"Gosh, fishhooks and everything," she whispered in what she hoped would be interpreted as awe.

"Open the plastic box on the left," Judd instructed. "That's the best one."

She read the label on the container. "Lazy Ike." The curved piece of bluish painted plastic didn't look anything like a small fish. The double branch of hooks did appear deadly, though.

Laura Lee inwardly shivered, wondering if fish would scream if they had vocal cords.

"Take it out of the box," Judd softly instructed.

Obeying, she gingerly removed the lure, careful not to touch the barbs of the six hooks. Her gray eyes filled with tears. There, lying in the bottom of the plastic box, was a solitaire diamond strung on a thin necklace of gold.

"It's gorgeous," she said sincerely. Wildly she flung her arms around her husband's neck. "You're the best husband in the world!"

Judd laughed with glee. "You were ready to stick every one of those hooks into me, weren't you?" he asked, then lifted her up in his arms as he kissed her awaiting mouth.

"Never," she protested when her feet touched the floor. "But you will have to teach me how to fish."

"You're a fast learner," he whispered for her ears only. "In six or eight months I'll have you griping that I don't take you fishing enough."

Laura Lee chuckled. She knew he was referring to how long it had taken him to get her into the bedroom and how she hadn't managed to mask her disappointment when Mac walked into their room.

"Some things take longer than others," she replied in a hushed voice, "unless, of course, you're comparing the thrill of going to bed with you with murdering some unsuspecting fish."

"We only have one thing in common," Judd said braggingly. "A big fish is called a whopper."

"Such modesty," she quipped, pinching his cheek between thumb and forefinger. "Get rid of Mac, and I'll let you prove it."

"Did I hear you say 'Get rid of Mac'?" Mac said. He had picked up her graphite rod and was whipping the tip back and forth. "Don't you want to try this beauty?"

Judd chuckled; Laura Lee blushed.

"That's what I had in mind, old buddy. Why don't you go rent the boat and we'll meet you at the dock."

"You aren't going to rent a boat here, are you? They get an arm and a leg at a resort. We need to scout out the other marinas first. You two can neck in the back seat, and I'll drive Laura Lee's car if you want to, but we need to get cracking."

Her back to Mac, still in Judd's strong arms, Laura Lee groaned audibly. The three of them were adults, but with her strict upbringing, asking Mac to leave while they made whoopee embarrassed her. Giving Judd a big hug, she said, "I'll change in the bathroom."

"You're a good sport," Mac said, complimenting her. He pointed his finger at Judd. "Not like other people in the room."

Judd watched Laura Lee take her swimsuit

out of the suitcase and close the bathroom door before he replied, "Mac, this is our honeymoon, not a boy's camping trip. I'm aware you and Vanessa have lived together for months, but we haven't. Every time my wife and I are in the mood to climb in bed I can count on you or Vanessa to arrive." He stepped closer, keeping his voice down. "What the hell is wrong with you?"

"Not me. Vanessa. Wrong time of the month for a honeymoon." Mac shrugged nonchalantly. "That's why she's so temperamental. You know how women are."

"I haven't been alone with my wife long enough to find out," Judd said huffily. He reached into his pocket and removed the car keys. Holding them out, he jangled them once. "You spend the rest of the morning searching for the best deal on renting a boat. My wife and I have other plans."

"But I thought it would be fun to . . ." Mac began protesting.

"Fun is here . . ."

Mac grabbed the keys. "I'll bet you'd go if Vanessa made the suggestion."

Judd opened his mouth to tell Mac what he thought of Vanessa's blatant suggestions but clamped his mouth shut. Mac would deny any allegation. He would defend his wife just as Judd knew he would knock the teeth down the throat of any man who maligned Laura Lee. Determined to defuse a potentially dangerous situation, Judd patted Mac on the shoulder and grinned.

"You're the one who persuaded me to make this trip a foursome." Appealing to his masculinity, he added with ribald humor, "I don't fish in another man's pond."

The frown on Mac's face changed into a smile. He patted Judd on the butt in a gesture reminiscent of their high school athletic days. "I know that. Vanessa is so damned beautiful she could convince a vegetarian to shout, 'Where's the beef?' "

Judd escorted his friend to the door and opened it. "Call before you come."

Nodding, sketching a military salute, Mac left.

Not leaving anything to chance, Judd locked the door and took the phone off the hook. Faster than a banana could be peeled, he shucked off his clothing. A grin of anticipation on his face, he slipped between the sheets of the nearest twin bed.

"I heard Mac leave," Laura Lee said as she opened the bathroom door. "Judd? What are you doing in bed?"

"What do you think I'm doing in bed? Waiting for my bride, of course," he answered triumphantly.

His brown eyes glowed as they flitted over the

bikini-clad curvaceous body stalking toward him. She gracefully crossed to the patio doors and pulled the drapes shut.

"Wouldn't want the pigeons to get any ideas," Laura Lee commented. The pile of clothes on the floor answered any question she had about his state of dress.

"The necklace becomes you. After I had bought it, I fantasized about seeing you wear it . . . and nothing else. Come over here, bride. I'm about to enact my fantasy."

Laura Lee fingered the bright diamond. "It's lovely, Judd."

"Mmmmmm. I hadn't noticed." Propped up on one arm, he added, "I did notice the beautiful setting, though. Maybe I ought to buy a longer chain. Then it will dangle, hidden in the shadow of your breasts."

Kneeling beside the bed, she framed his face with both hands. "Did I remember to thank you properly for the gifts?"

Judd reached behind her and unsnapped the top of her swimsuit. His hand warmly cupped the underside of her breast gently before he removed the cloth barrier. His hand agilely unhooked the sides of the bottoms.

"No. I don't believe you did."

She covered his lips with her own possessively. One hand swept the bedclothes aside. With the knowledge of what pleased Judd the most, she caressed him intimately. His tongue swirled inside her mouth as he groaned from low in his throat. His strong arm wrapped around her waist and pulled her on top of him.

"Thank you," she crooned.

"You're welcome," Judd answered with a smile. "Twin beds require creative positioning."

Laura Lee put a knee on each side of his upper thighs and sat back. "The aerial view from up here is great."

"I was thinking the same thing." Gently he circled her nipples with sensitive fingers. "Mount Venus."

"The Great Plains," she replied, raking her hands over his broad chest.

Playfully Judd drew a line from her collarbone to her navel. "Grand Canyon."

"Redwood Forest," she replied, tugging at the hair on his chest.

Judd laughed huskily as his fingers delved below her waist. "Wrong. That's part of your map, not mine."

"Geography isn't my forte," she said. "You're bawdy, Mr. Simpson."

Laura Lee fought against closing her eyes but couldn't. Much as she loved watching his expressive face, she wanted to let touch be her dominant sense. Her breasts flattened against his chest. Sensually she raised her shoulders and let the sensitive tips brush against him.

"Kiss me," he demanded hoarsely.

Passionately their lips fused. His tongue parodied his surging finger. She rotated her hips joyously, unhampered by the weight of his body. Using his other hand, he slowly guided her to receive him.

Laura Lee sipped thirstily at his tongue until she felt his hands on her shoulders lift her away.

"Open your silver eyes," he whispered. "The dark centers envelop me the way you do, drawing me into their passionate center."

As though drugged, she opened her eyes a millimeter. Through the tips of her lashes she saw the intense concentration on his dark features.

"Raise up some more."

She stiffened her arms, locking her elbows to support her weight. Judd held her close enough for him to caress her breasts lovingly. First with his hands, then with the hot moistness of his mouth, he aroused her to incredible heights.

The passion built like a fiery ball in her belly. Judd increased the suckling on her breasts as though he wanted her to be as deeply embedded as he was. The fury of his lovemaking was volcanic. With rapture only seconds away, she frantically moved her hips. Nothing could stop her from attaining her quest.

When spasmodically the heated ball exploded, she squeezed her eyes shut. Sparks of pure color painted a wild picture in front of her eyes. Spiraling bolts of red, blue, yellow, green spun together in untamed abandon.

"Judd!" she called, clutching his shoulders, fearing she would lose her balance in the throes of her climax.

He arched his hips for one powerful thrust as he, too, exploded, clamping her hips to receive the force of his eruption.

Collapsing against him, Laura Lee panted kisses against the strong column of his neck. He held her so closely she felt in danger of having her ribs cracked. But she wouldn't have known or cared. Ripples of pleasure were the side effect of their loving.

"We're going to have to put limits on your abilities." Judd breathed heavily. "I feel as weak as a newborn kitten."

"Loving you is the closest thing to heaven," Laura Lee whispered.

Chuckling at her extravagance, Judd kissed her damp brow. "Close to perfect," he said smugly. "I hope I have the strength to throw a fishing lure in the water."

"We could stay here and rest."

Using her fingers, she playfully walked across his chest, up his throat to his carved lips. *This is the way a honeymoon should be spent,* she mused. *Wrapped around each other, lazily ex-*

ploring the depths of passion rather than searching the lake for cold-blooded fish.

"I'll work up the strength."

"But I can think of a better way to expend it," Laura Lee said suggestively.

"Not with the gruesome twosome pounding on the door!"

"Why, Judd Simpson, am I hearing criticism of your favorite couple of the month?"

Laughing, Judd gave her bottom a gentle smack. "Be good."

"Wasn't I?"

"Mmmmmmm. Fantastic, but . . ." Judd got up and crossed to the bathroom. "Let's go try out your new equipment."

Laura Lee pulled the sheet up over her head. "I think I'll catch some shut-eye."

"And I think you'll slip into that scanty bikini of yours and catch some crappie."

Crappie, she silently moaned. *Appropriate name for our upcoming activity.*

"Do I have to get back in bed and persuade you?"

Folding the sheet off her head, she smiled beguilingly. "Convince me!"

Judd reentered the room, laughing. "You're inexhaustible, aren't you?"

"Yep. Ain't it great?" With a cheeky smile she curved her body seductively and lowered the

106

sheet to her waist. "See the monster you created."

"Unlike Frankenstein's, my gorgeous red-headed creation is controlled by keeping her satisfied in bed." Judd tapped his temple. "Clever planning, don't you think?"

"Very clever, Dr. Frankenstein. But remember how the story ended?"

Leaning over, Judd brushed the loose flame-colored curls off her face. "The monster killed the doctor. I can see it all now." He panned his hand as though he were a movie director. "Monster Simpson chases the good doctor around the hotel room. She catches him. Oh-oh. What's she doing? Oh, no! She has a strangling hug on his neck. Watch out, Doctor. She's going to . . ." Judd shook his head in mock dejection. "Poor guy. Killed him with love."

Laura Lee picked up her pillow and slung it toward his head. Laughing, Judd blocked the oncoming object with his forearm.

"You should be so lucky."

"That's my first name: Lucky Judd Simpson. But only since our wedding day."

"Guess we both changed our names, huh?"

His lips hummed in agreement as he sweetly kissed her. "You have two minutes to get dressed."

"Last night I had two minutes to get dressed

. . . in my nightgown. I think I prefer your nighttime orders better."

Judd reached down and picked up her swimsuit. "Do I have to dress you?"

"That would be unique. I can remember a time when all you wanted to do was *un*dress me. Married life sure does change a man," she retorted with a smiling pout.

Judd dropped her suit and swiftly removed his trunks. "Never let it be said I changed the moment the vows were spoken. Move over, woman."

CHAPTER SIX

"I thought you had to get up at sunrise to catch fish," Laura Lee commented as she pushed the button on her reel too soon. The Lazy Ike plunked into the water behind her shoulder.

With a smug smile Vanessa cast. Her lure landed without a splash two feet from the bank. "These are vacation fish. They spend the morning sleeping in, mating."

"Clever fish," Laura Lee quipped with a low chuckle.

Vanessa had been needling her for the past hour, but Laura Lee was determined not to let her get under her skin. Secretly she hoped the fish stayed away from her lure. Although she had watched her archrival triumphantly hog in six fish, she had also watched her remove the fish from the triple hooks. There was little doubt in her mind that both the crappie and the fisherman, or in this case fisherwoman, would be hooked the first time it flopped.

"Ten, two, ten o'clock." Judd instructed her

patiently. "You can't catch them if you don't cast properly."

"You noticed," Laura Lee muttered. "I think I'll reel this dude in and take a nap on the back cushions. Why don't you join me?"

"And let Vanessa and Mac catch more fish than we do?"

Mac began vigorously reeling. "Got another one!"

Whoopee. Laura Lee silently congratulated him. *Ten, two, ten o'clock.* "Hey, I did it!" The Lazy Ike cartwheeled end over end as it arched toward the bank.

"Jerk it back!" Judd shouted.

Like an acrobat, the lure wrapped itself repeatedly around a low-slung branch on a willow tree edging the bank. Laura Lee's head rotated in a matching motion. The more tightly she tugged backward, the faster it spun around.

"Too late?" she asked with a nervous giggle. The three of them were glaring at her as though she had committed a heinous crime.

"No crappie in the trees," Vanessa sarcastically answered. "Hand the rod over here, and I'll get it loose for you."

"I can get it," Laura Lee said. She whipped the tip of the rod backward. The lure dangled from the limb in pendulum motion. "Could we move over there so I can unwrap it?" she asked.

"We're sitting on a gold hole. If we pull the

110

anchor up, the fish will scatter like leaves in a strong wind. Hand the butt of the rod over here."

Laura Lee did as Judd instructed. Unable to reach his outstretched hand with the grip, she grabbed the tip end of the rod.

"Don't grab the—"

The limber, fragile tip snapped off in her hand. The black handle banged into the bottom of the boat.

"—tip." Judd finished his instructions too late.

"You broke it." Mac wailed as though she had murdered his best friend.

Surprised, Laura Lee lurched to her feet. The boat shifted precariously with her sudden movement. She plopped back down on the cushion to keep herself from being pitched overboard. She saved herself, but the loud, high-pitched squeal told her someone else hadn't been as lucky.

"Vanessa!" Mac yelled, jumping overboard.

"Get a life jacket," Judd shouted as he maneuvered to the back of the boat. "Vanessa doesn't swim."

"Doesn't swim?" Panicked, Laura Lee jumped off the bench. The boat pitched to the left, then violently rocked to the right. She grabbed the side of the boat and held on for dear life. Although Judd had braced himself by spreading his weight equally on both feet, he wasn't prepared for the abrupt shifting. He, too, catapulted out of the bass boat.

Laura Lee screamed when she heard the cannonball splash. In less than three minutes she had dumped everyone out of the boat. She did have the presence of mind to open the bench seat and throw all the flotation devices overboard. How was she to know the victims of her inexperience were on the other side of the boat?

"She did it on purpose!" Vanessa screamed, sputtering and spitting.

"Let go of my neck," Mac shouted.

Laura Lee could hear his loud gurgling as his head sank beneath the surface of the water. Her gray eyes widened in fear. They all were going to drown, and it was her fault. Knees shaking, she climbed to the back deck. The last rational thought she had as she plunged into the chilled water was: *Thank God I was a lifeguard.*

"Get away from me. Help! Help! She's trying to drown me."

"Judd? Judd?" Laura Lee called the moment she surfaced.

"Coming."

Mac's hand grabbed for air as he went under for the third time.

"You get Vanessa . . . I'll get Mac," Judd shouted. "Let go, Vanessa. You're drowning him."

"Nooooooo. Save me, Mac!"

"Get back," Laura Lee shouted at Judd. Vanessa, frightened of drowning herself, didn't realize she was holding her husband's head under the water. There was only one thing to do according to the lifesaving techniques Laura Lee had been taught. After drawing her fist back, she belted Vanessa in the jaw. Immediately Vanessa released Mac. Laura Lee told Judd, "Grab him."

Laura Lee swam to the back side of Vanessa and grabbed a handful of her hair. With even strokes she began hauling her back by the hair on her head.

"Ooooouch! Let go of my hair!"

"You'll drown," Laura Lee sputtered. "I'm saving you."

"You're pulling my hair out by the roots!"

"Shut up, Vanessa. Quit fighting me, or I'll pop you again."

By the time she managed to get to the side of the boat Judd had already hauled Mac into the boat. Hacking and coughing, Mac cleared the water from his lungs. Judd braced himself against the side of the boat, leaned over, and plucked a screaming Vanessa out of the water.

"She hit me," Vanessa complained. "And pulled my hair!"

"I saved your life," Laura Lee protested as she heaved herself into the boat. "Is Mac okay?"

"You're a disaster walking around looking for

a place to happen," Vanessa squawked, fending Laura Lee away from Mac.

Judd dug beneath the driver's seat and pulled out four towels. "You okay?" he ask as he tossed Laura Lee a towel.

Shaking her head positively, she attempted to kneel down in the bottom of the boat to check Mac out. The boat began shifting back and forth. *Oh, no, not again,* she protested silently.

Judd righted the boat and hauled Laura Lee onto the bench. "Sit there. Please."

"She's trying to kill us all," Vanessa screeched.

"I've never been in a bass boat before. I told you that. All of you," Laura Lee explained. "I've only been in big ski boats."

"You did it on purpose. You don't like to fish, so you tried to drown us. And you pitched us overboard with our rods and reels. We couldn't fish now if we wanted to," Vanessa said, berating her.

Mac sat up and belched loudly, drawing everyone's attention. "You almost became a widow."

"It was her fault," Vanessa cried, pointing her finger toward Laura Lee.

"I didn't do it on purpose," the accused protested.

"She did. She hit me. I'll bet my whole face is purple on one side."

"Only your jaw," Mac observed.

"And she tried to snatch me bald!"

"It was the only way I could get you back to the boat. You would have drowned me, too!"

"Good," Vanessa shouted vindictively.

"Everybody calm down!" Judd shouted over the bickering, which threatened to become violent. "It was an accident. Laura Lee didn't mean to knock anybody out of the boat."

Vanessa snorted.

Mac coughed.

Laura Lee gave each of them a weak smile of apology.

"I'll gather up what remains of our fishing equipment, and we'll head back. Don't anybody move," Judd sternly instructed, looking directly at his bride.

"I want to ski," Vanessa protested.

"Ski? You dumb bunny. You can't even swim," Laura Lee said without compunction.

"That's what ski jackets are for. And don't you call me a dumb bunny, you . . . potential murderess!"

"Shut up!" Judd shouted over the ensuing verbal battle.

Silence reigned while he pulled up the anchor and used the long-poled net to gather in the life jackets. Vanessa shot silent knives in Laura Lee's direction. Mac eased himself up beside his wife and draped his arm around her shoulders.

You'd think I planned this catastrophe, Laura

Lee fumed, shades of guilt washing over her face. Maybe, unintentionally, subconsciously she had. It certainly had put an abrupt halt to the fishing expedition. She glanced at the tree that had precipitated the whole fiasco and her broken rod. No, she thought, acquitting herself. It *was* an accident.

When she turned her eyes toward Vanessa, she winced. There was a bluish purple mark along the side of her jaw. Silently she quizzed herself. *Could I have made her let Mac's head loose without decking her? Could I have hit her with less force? Did I use the excuse of Mac's drowning to clobber Vanessa to repay her for all the little digs she's made?* Had the "small fish" revolted against the tyranny of the "big fish"?

Laura Lee covered her mouth with her hand to hide a smile. *You're naughty, Mrs. Laura Lee Simpson.* She chastised herself, not feeling the least bit bad. *If some little girl had smacked Vanessa in the mouth at a tender age, it probably would have resulted in her growing up to be a nicer person.*

She doubted that one quick punch in the chops to save her life would correct Vanessa's personality problems. *Too little, too late,* Laura Lee thought, completely vindicating herself of the incident.

"You want to drive?" Judd asked Laura Lee when he had completed his cleanup tasks.

"Don't let her drive," Mac protested with a laugh. "We'll end up decorating the bluffs."

To answer Judd's question, she mutely shook her head. Her gray eyes pleaded for understanding. "I'll come up and sit by you, though."

"Noooooo!" Vanessa squeaked, clamping her arms around a life jacket. "You'll dump us again."

Judd extended his hand in his wife's direction. "No quick movements. Take my hand and slowly rise. That's a girl." He praised her once she had managed to sit beside him.

She wrapped her arm around his bare shoulder and spoke quietly into his ear. "They're angry."

Laughing at her understatement, Judd replied, "Once they get the water out of their lungs, they'll be in a better mood. You did warn us when Mac showed us the boat that you had never been out in a bass boat."

"They laughed, remember?"

"They aren't laughing now."

Glancing over her arm, she saw the two of them scowling at her. "No sense of humor."

"We'll eat a late lunch. Maybe food will improve their disposition."

Snuggling closer, Laura Lee didn't care whether or not their disposition improved. She hadn't invited them on her honeymoon. As far as she was concerned, she hoped they stayed mad.

The engine roared to life when Judd twisted the key. Unable to communicate without yelling, she rested her head on his muscular shoulder and began hatching plots to dissociate Mac and Vanessa from their honeymoon.

How about if I made a wild play for Mac? Vanessa would be furious. Furious enough to haul Mac up to their plush suite possessively? Not a bad idea, but how would Judd react? Bad idea, she deduced. *He would be in a snit for hours.* Besides, there was something basically repugnant about outrageously flirting with another man on her own honeymoon. The only person's attention she wanted was her husband's.

I could plead a violent headache. Judd would solicitously take me up to our pigeon roost and . . . Silently chuckling, she saw real merit in this plan. Mentally she pictured Judd escorting her to the room, but once there, powee, faster than a speeding bullet, with Wonder Woman strength, she'd tackle him. He'd land on the bed . . . *and with your luck, he would hit his head on the headboard, have a concussion, and spend the night in the hospital.*

She rejected the idea. How had Judd managed to have her do the bedroom manipulating? Before they were married, he had been the one to concoct a thousand excuses to slip between the sheets. Now that they were married, she was the one stretching her imagination to the hilt.

Did the roles reverse with all newlyweds? Was the chase over for the male and therefore required less effort on his part? Once the ring had been placed on the bride's finger did the groom shout, "She's mine anytime I want her," and immediately lose interest?

That isn't true, she admonished herself. Judd hadn't lost interest. An ugly thought niggled forward from the back of her mind: *He's plenty interested when he wants to get his way in a dispute.* He had managed to talk her into doubling on their honeymoon by caressing a "yes" through her defiant lips. He had changed the destination of their trip the same way, hadn't he? And today he had convinced her she would love fishing . . . after they had spent several hours in bed.

Mentally she installed a warning bell in her subconscious. Each time Judd won a battle by making the bed the battleground, the alarm would ring. If this were going to be a trend, she would have to change her behavior pattern. Wanton behavior—was it typical of a straitlaced bride? Everything was legal. Once the binding restraints of society had been removed, had she gone a bit wild? She couldn't help smiling. Judd certainly approved of her "wildness." Any fear she had harbored about his disliking an assertive woman in the bedroom had been swiftly abolished. He relished her active participation!

When the rush of wind caused by the speeding boat dwindled, Laura Lee opened her eyes. Instead of coming up with a workable idea to get rid of the couple in the back seat, she had unwisely diverted her thoughts to the problem hiding beneath the surface of their marriage. As her eyes scanned the half-empty dock, she realized Judd was conducting an obedience school training course and she was blithely following his commands.

No more, she vowed. He was going to have to assume the role of coaxing lover, or she would get a violent headache—one that would drastically curtail her desire. Just because she had taken the traditional pledge to love, honor, and obey, that didn't mean she had automatically been converted into a mindless bride. Removing her arm, scooting inches away, she closed her mind to the sensual delights Judd evoked simply by brushing his arm inconspicuously against the side of her breast. By golly, if he could be casual about when and how often they went to bed, so could she. Time to get his anxiety level up, she declared. *Let him wonder how he's going to get me into bed instead of vice versa!*

"Grab hold of the dock," Judd instructed as he

slowly maneuvered the boat into the narrow dock.

Yes, indeedy, she thought, *he can grab hold of his own dock!*

"Let me out of here," Vanessa ordered as she clambered onto the dock. "Safe, at last."

The meaningful look she shot in Laura Lee's direction wasn't missed by any of them. The wind had blown her wet peroxided hair into a helter-skelter mess of brittle knots. Her hands patted through it as though trying to restore it to a sophisticated upsweep. When she removed them, nature must have laughed as the coarse strands openly rebelled by sticking straight out. If a hunter had seen her in the forest, Laura Lee thought, he wouldn't know whether to tag her, shoot her, or run away.

"How about a late lunch and a long, cool drink?" Judd offered politely.

"Sounds good to me," Mac accepted without reservation.

"Hold the boat while Laura Lee gets out, would you?" Judd's whole face smiled. Nothing tragic had happened. True, they had taken an unexpected dip, and Vanessa's carefully made-up face and hair had suffered along with her dignity, but none of them was permanently injured.

Brown eyes glowing, he watched his wife gracefully take Mac's hand and spring from the

121

seat of the boat. On the way back he had specu-
lated about the possibility of his sweet bride's
intentionally splatting Vanessa into the lake. He
could almost see her telling Vanessa to take a
flying leap and then assisting her on the journey.
She, without a doubt, was one of the feistiest
women he had ever encountered. *And she's
mine,* he thought, his smile widening. *Mine to
tame with love.*

The urge to touch the sensitive backs of her
knees, casually to help her out of the boat while
thoroughly enjoying the chore made him rise to
his feet. Laura Lee used the boat for leverage as
she bound upward. For a moment she straddled
a wide space of water. Then Mac yanked harder,
and both feet touched the dock.

She turned around just in time to see Judd
waving his arms frantically in an effort to gain
his balance. *Not again.* She moaned. Judd
caught hold of the opposite side of the dock. The
boat immediately started to drift back in her
direction. Stooping down, she shoved the boat
back under Judd's sprawling body. Within seconds Judd had recovered enough balance to
spring onto the dock.

"Disaster lady," Vanessa mumbled. She
started to shake her frizzled head but instead
reached into her shorts pocket and pulled out a
damp head scarf. With practiced ease she made
a voguish turban.

"Accidents do happen," Judd stated defensively.

Vanessa stuck out her bruised jaw. "This was no accident. She hit me as hard as she could."

"She may have saved your life," Judd parried. "I had my hands full with Mac . . . whom you almost drowned."

"Let's eat lunch. There is no point in rehashing the incident," Mac suggested, playing the role of peacemaker.

"You agree with him," Vanessa said accusingly. "I suppose I should be grateful that you didn't hit me."

"I don't strike women," Mac stated unequivocally. "Regardless of how damaging to my own health the principle is."

"Mac McDougal. You wanted to hit me, too! My own husband wants to hit me," she wailed loudly enough to attract the attention of anyone on the boat dock.

Mac rolled his eyes to the heavens as though asking for patience. "If she falls in again, will you save her . . . the same way?" Mac asked Laura Lee with a grimace. "I missed the last punch, but I'm beginning to think she needs a purple mark on the other side of her beautiful face."

"Well! Mr. McDougal, you can take a long walk off a short pier!" Having had the last word, Vanessa pivoted and stalked off the dock.

"You should go after her," Judd advised.

"She's in shock. Don't let this accident ruin your honeymoon."

Mac ignored Judd. In short, quick steps, he followed his wife's suggestion and plunged off the end of the dock. With long, sure strokes he broke the surface of the water and began swimming toward the small island off the point.

"Now there is a man I admire. He follows his wife's orders down to dotting the *i*'s, crossing the *t*'s, and taking a swim." Laura Lee laughed with unrestrained glee.

"You're terrible," Judd said scoldingly. His baritone laughter joined her trebled glee.

"So are you."

"Want to go be terrible together?" He gave her a villainous leer and rubbed his hands together in anticipation.

Laura Lee didn't hesitate. Twirling an imaginary mustache and wiggling her eyebrows, she answered, "Last one to the pigeon roost is a goose egg!"

Of course, my newly installed alarm didn't ring, she thought as she sprinted up the hill. *He isn't going to make love to me to get something other than pure, glorious physical satisfaction, and this time he's chasing me.* What more could a bride ask for? Determined to make him chase her the entire way, she lengthened her stride.

CHAPTER SEVEN

Clothed in a bright, sun-loving, summer-cool, lace-splashed green dress, Laura Lee felt like the radiant honeymooner she was. She waited for Judd to pull out the dining-room chair. Her silvery, happy eyes quickly surveyed the room. Mac and Vanessa weren't there. Giving an inward sigh of relief, she lowered herself onto the plush cushion.

"Did I tell you how fantastic you look, Mrs. Simpson?" Judd complimented her softly as he pushed her chair in. "Green is definitely your color."

Judd could make her believe she was the most gorgeous woman on earth with a certain look he gave her, but the verbal compliments warmed the glow on her cheeks. "I'm merely trying to keep up with the most handsome man in the Ozarks."

As he seated himself, then ordered a drink for each of them, his dark eyes proudly watched his lovely wife. Tonight there was a softness about her that appealed to his male instincts. It was hard to believe this soft, feminine creature had smacked someone hard enough to leave a bruise. That same hand had left a burning trail of butterfly touches all over his body. There wouldn't be any visible prints, but she continued to knock him off his feet with her eagerness to please. Her willingness to experiment invariably left him eager to reclaim her hastily as his own.

"A spicy dish," he murmured aloud.

"Chicken jambalaya?"

"Mrs. Judd Simpson is the spicy dish," Judd said praisingly.

When he raised his glass of wine in a silent toast, Laura Lee felt her hunger pangs diminish. He had awakened an insatiable appetite she had difficulty controlling. If Judd were fattening, she would weigh a ton, she thought.

Minuscule bubbles of effervescence tickled her nose. "Champagne? What else did you order?"

"Lobster, baked potato oozing with sour cream, strawberries dipped in Grand Marnier and coated with milk chocolate—"

"Stop!" Laura Lee protested. "You certainly know how to tempt your wife's palate, don't you?"

"Ummmmm-hmmmmm," he replied with a

self-satisfied grin. "You're particularly fond of desserts, but you usually refuse them. Why?"

Laura Lee laughed happily. "You would object to a less-than-trim wife, wouldn't you?"

He picked up her hand and nibbled kisses on each fingertip before answering. "Eat as much as you like. I'll think of a way to burn off the calories."

"You're one diet I'm never going to get tired of." The tiny kisses were sending delicate signals to her heartstrings, and they hummed a joyful tune in response. "You take my breath away, make my heart want to sing."

"Wicked little ditties?"

"Ones that couldn't be sung in polite company," she admitted with an impish smile.

"Like the one you gustily sang in the shower. I haven't heard that rendition since I was at a fraternity party. Where did you learn all those verses?"

Shrugging, a pink tinge flowing over her high cheekbones, she chuckled. "I guess there are still a lot of things we don't know about each other."

"Something tells me being married to you is going to be fun spelled in all capital letters."

"Is marriage supposed to be boring?" she quipped, delighted that he found her intriguing.

"Some are. I hate to admit this, but I thought

you were beginning to take me for granted yesterday."

"Yesterday?" she repeated, puzzled.

"When Vanessa was practicing her wiles on me. You acted as though you didn't have a thing to worry about."

"Did I?"

"No, but—"

"Why, Mr. Simpson, I do believe you wanted me to throw a jealous tantrum."

Judd cleared his throat uncomfortably. "I expected you to protect your property."

"You aren't my property, any more than I'm your property."

"I defended you today when a certain unmentionable party had her talons spread ready to strike."

"And I appreciated it, but that's different. On one hand, you protected me from bodily harm; on the other hand, you wanted me to inflict bodily harm."

Chuckling, Judd retorted, "You did a bit of that also."

"But not with malice intended." The picture of innocence, she sipped her wine. "Don't raise your eyebrow at me. You know I had to make her let go of Mac."

"I seem to remember from my lifesaving class that the rescuer pulls the victim under the water until she lets go."

"Are you siding with her? Do you really think I . . ." Laura Lee left the question dangling. "You do! You think I knocked her out of the boat on purpose and compounded the crime by beating up on her once she was in the water."

Judd loved playing the devil's advocate. Watching her eyes shoot silver bullets in his direction confirmed his belief of there being plenty of action in their marriage. He shrugged as though he weren't certain what he believed.

"I didn't know she couldn't swim," Laura Lee said in defense of her actions. "She does every other sport to perfection. How was I to know she wouldn't be attempting to drown me instead of its being the other way around?"

"Aha! You admitted it. You said you attempted to drown Vanessa."

Cocking her head to one side, she asked, "Did I say that?"

Judd laughed aloud at the puzzled expression on her face. It was seldom that he won any verbal arguments; he had to resort to bedroom tactic to guarantee a win. Under the table he shifted to the side to dodge the tip of her evening shoe.

"I must be slipping," Laura Lee whispered, leaning forward so the deep V of her neckline distracted Judd. "I usually don't miss with my mouth or my foot."

"A delightful refreshing change. Who knows,

maybe I won't resort to winning our battles in the bedroom if I can win a few verbal skirmishes," he said jokingly with halfhearted sincerity.

The waiter's bringing the first course of their dinner allowed for a change in topic. Neither of them wanted to let the boating incident mar being completely alone with the other. Judd found himself drawn closer and closer to his wife. She was as enticing, as beguiling, as tantalizing a bride as she had been during their courtship. He might have wanted certain things to change in their lovemaking, as they had, but there were diamond-clear facets of his wife he wanted to remain unchangeable.

After they had finished the main course and polished off the strawberries, they relaxed contentedly and drank coffee laced with brandy.

"Are you getting tipsy, my dear wife?" Judd huskily asked when she discreetly took off her shoe and began sliding her nylon-clad toes up his ankles.

"Ladies never overindulge." She unlaced her fingers from between his and slipped them beneath the white linen tablecloth.

"Stop. We have company."

The curt instructions halted her adventuresome finger. Judd's rising to his feet dislodged them completely.

Laura Lee jammed her foot back into her

shoe. "Mr. and Mrs. McDougal, I presume?" she grunted in unladylike tones.

"Join us," Judd invited graciously.

Go away, Laura Lee groaned silently while mustering up a false smile.

"We don't want to interrupt," Mac said, starting to refuse.

"Nonsense. I'll have the waiter bring another bottle of champagne," Judd offered, motioning to the waiter by raising the empty bottle in the silver champagne bucket.

"Well, if you insist," Vanessa cooed, slipping into the chair adjacent to Judd's. "We've made a decision."

"Let's have some wine before we tell them our *suggestion*," Mac said. Laura Lee glanced at him under half-veiled eyelashes. Mac looked as though he had been pulled through a knothole, backward. Whatever decision Vanessa had arbitrarily made, it wasn't sitting well on Mac's hunched shoulders.

Efficiently the waiter set crystal stemware in front of each of their guests. Judd nodded, indicating the suitability of the wine, and the steward poured each glass half full.

Raising his glass, Judd toasted, "To our beautiful brides."

Mac clinked his champagne glass against Judd's, but the tone was hollow. He didn't add to or show enthusiasm about the toast. His eyes skittered back and forth between Judd and Laura Lee.

"'And to the men in our lives," Vanessa added glibly.

Laura Lee wasn't certain, but she thought Mac visually winced at the amendment to the toast. *Poor Mac,* she found herself thinking for the umpteenth time.

"To my man," Laura Lee said, stipulating lovingly, "my husband."

"Of course," Vanessa said civilly.

They each took a sip, except for Mac. He tossed the wine down as though it were fortification for what was about to take place.

"Tell them, darling," Vanessa said coaxingly.

She's about as subtle as a cattle prod, Laura Lee thought. The champagne before dinner had had a sweetness; this wine tasted like straight, undiluted vinegar.

"We want to go back to Kansas City," Mac stated bluntly.

Judd glanced at the horrified expression on his wife's face, then asked in a dangerously soft tone, "Why? Our reservations are for the entire week. Our deposit also, I might add."

"What's a couple of hundred dollars? This vacation has been jinxed from the moment we left the city." Vanessa patted Mac on the shoulder as though he had been a good little boy.

"I'm sorry you feel that way. There aren't any

planes that fly into the Ozarks, or any trains. Have you checked out the bus schedule?" Laura Lee asked sweetly, knowing full well Vanessa wouldn't be caught dead on a Greyhound bus.

"A bus? You're kidding," she protested expectedly. Reaching across the table, she squeezed Laura Lee's hand and giggled as though they were sharing a hilarious joke. "I don't take public transportation."

Laura Lee flipped her hand over and returned the bone-smashing grip. "Hope you brought your hiking shoes," she glibly replied. "I have no intention of cutting my honeymoon short to drive you back to K.C. in my car."

Appealing to Judd, Vanessa fluttered her false eyelashes in his direction. "You wouldn't let your best friend and his wife walk back to Kansas City, would you?"

"Of course not," Judd replied. He felt the spike of his wife's heel on the toe of his shoe. "But let's not be hasty about departing." The pressure decreased. "We've had a few minor—"

"Disasters," Vanessa inserted. "I spent the first night in a hovel twenty miles from the lake. Today, thanks to sweet little innocent Laura Lee, I nearly drowned." Sarcasm coated each word like sugar on an M&M. "We're leaving before total disaster strikes."

"Care to trade rooms?" Laura Lee suggested. "Maybe the king-size water bed is soaking your brain. We have lovely twin beds . . . with an iron bar to keep them apart. And our view from the pigeon poop balcony is fabulous. My heart weeps for you."

She could have bitten her tongue for the smart-assed retaliation. Rather than unload Vanessa's weapon, she had provided her with more deadly ammunition. Antagonizing Vanessa wasn't the way to make her change her mind.

"Exactly," Vanessa said, crowing. "I have it all figured out so we won't lose our deposit. Mac and Judd will go to the manager and tell him we've run out of money. The deposit can pay for last night and tonight."

"How am I going to explain the hundred-dollar bills being kept for me in the deposit vault?"

"You gave the hotel all your money?" Vanessa asked in disbelief.

Judd nodded. "I didn't have time to go to the bank and get traveler's checks. When I made the room deposit and registered, I gave them all the large bills. Safety precaution."

"I'll reimburse you for the deposit on the room," Mac offered.

"Money is not the point," Laura Lee protested. "I don't want to return home early." She enunciated each word distinctly as though speaking to a group of mentally deficient children. "You go; we'll stay."

"I told you she would be selfish," Vanessa

whined. Magically, tears trickled down her rouged cheeks. "Tomorrow we could be assassinated. Or the boat could explode. Or—"

Mac loudly sighed. Palms raised in a gesture of defeat, he appealed to Judd's good nature.

Don't let them manipulate you, Laura Lee warned by increasing the pressure of her heel.

"You're upset, Vanessa," Judd said placatingly. "Why don't we discuss this in the morning when you've slept on it?"

Sympathy isn't what she needs. Laura Lee fumed, clenching her fist. When Vanessa drooped like a wilted flower on Judd's forearm, Laura Lee's restraint snapped.

"Get off my husband!" Laura Lee snarled. "I've had it up to here"—her hand slashed a mark above eye level—"with your crap!"

The volume of Vanessa's tears increased, as did the keening wail from her lips.

"Ladies, you're making a scene," Mac said in reaction. His finger dug at the space between his starched white collar and beet red neck, but the extra space didn't stop the red tide that swept over his tanned features. "Knock it off, Laura Lee."

"Don't say that!" Judd cautioned.

"I'm not going to clobber your blushing bride," Laura Lee informed Mac icily. "I'm quietly going to get up from the table, go to my room . . . and scream the roof down!"

True to her word, she stood, smiled, and exited.

Laura Lee prided herself on controlling her redhead's temper. The idea of making a scene in a restaurant was abhorrent to her. Mac and Judd could work the problem out. Or . . . *Judd can walk back to Kansas City with them,* she thought angrily.

So I'm selfish, she added silently with a snort. *I object to cutting my weeklong honeymoon to two nights, and I'm selfish?* When it came to name-calling, Vanessa had hidden her iron fist with a velvet glove, but Laura Lee wasn't fooled. Vanessa would manipulate and wheedle until both men felt lower than bugs beneath a toadstool.

Poor Mac, she thought sympathetically. Talk about being caught between a rock and a hard spot. His choices were more limited than her own. At least when they did return home, she wouldn't have to see Vanessa's face again. *And I won't,* she promised herself.

The thought made her stop in her tracks outside their pigeon roost.

"I blew it," she stated aloud. "I'm up here . . . alone and Vanessa is down there, soaking up sympathy. Judd mistakenly suspects I did cause the accident on purpose. Will he agree to . . ."

She couldn't voice her fear. Judd wouldn't do

136

that. He wanted to vacation for a few more days, too, she thought reasonably. As though to dismiss the thought from her mind totally, she vigorously shook her head.

After taking the key from her purse, she unlocked the door and entered. The moon shed a surrealistic light into the room. Nothing seemed real. This couldn't be happening. Not to her. Not on her honeymoon.

Vanessa wasn't the only one who felt like crying. Laura Lee wanted to fling herself down on the twin bed and sob her eyes out. But she didn't. Stiffening her jaw, thrusting it forward, she was determined not to lose faith in her husband's ability to do what was best, what was right.

Mentally she tried to strike the past half hour from her memory and think about the lovely dinner for two they had shared. Judd could charm the birds from the trees when he set his mind to it. Hadn't she seen him do it that time a customer had been presented a check for his dinner when he hadn't been served yet? Judd could cajole Mac into growing a backbone, couldn't he?

Laura Lee slumped on the bed. *Backbones don't come easily,* she thought. But maybe he could mesmerize Vanessa into changing her mind. Slowly she began unzipping her dress.

Who would win the battle taking place in the

dining room? Vanessa with her woeful tears? Judd with his captivating smile? Mac? Again she pitied Mac.

"I should have stayed to help Judd convince them." She berated herself aloud. "No one should fight my battles but me."

Too late, she realized. They were hashing through the problem, and she was alone in a dark room, taking off her clothes. Vanessa had warned her to be the trainer instead of the trainee. Watching Mac request cutting their honeymoon short certainly validated her claim of being the deciding force in their new household. What totally amazed Laura Lee was Vanessa's ability to tread up and down Mac's back, squashing his backbone to smithereens, and for him to gaze adoringly at her as though she could do no wrong.

If I pulled something like that, Judd would . . . What would Judd do? Laura Lee grimaced. "After he picked his teeth up off the floor, he'd jam them down my throat," she said aloud.

Not true, the devil lurking in her subconscious argued. *Resorting to violence isn't the method he uses. He whispers sweet nothings in your ear, distracts you from rational thought via the bed, then convinces you to do things his way.*

When the door opened and Judd entered, she mentally armed herself for his subtle form of warfare.

"What are you doing sitting in the dark?" Judd asked. He turned on the bedside lamp and sat down beside her. "Mac has his hands full, doesn't he?"

"Quite the opposite," Laura Lee replied succinctly.

"They both are miserable," he informed her unnecessarily. When he drew her into his arms, they both fell back onto the bed. "You're wonderful. I don't have to put up with irrational behavior from you. I love you, Mrs. Simpson."

Here it comes. Her warning bell went off. *A dash of sweet talk, a pinch of lovemaking, and snap-o, instant capitulation. Why don't you follow his recipe for a change?*

"You're too masterful to let someone boss you around the way Vanessa does. Too masculine, too—"

"Stubborn?" Judd said teasingly.

He's doing it! Making you laugh, driving you wild with his marauding fingers. The devilish voice of her subconscious giving a commentary on Judd's technique kept her normal reaction—unbridled desire—under control.

She wiggled away from him. Judd rolled to his side. Laura Lee steeled herself against his lips as they softly covered hers. *Gentle persuasion,* the inner devil said workingly. *Not this time,* she promised herself. *Mac isn't the only one who needs to sprout a backbone.*

139

Her hands on his shoulders, she gave a negligible push. "Judd, I'm not going back to Kansas City. I can't resist your charming bedside manner, but regardless of how convincing you are, I'm not cutting our trip short."

"Come here, love. Your skin is cold. Let me warm you."

"You cannot solve problems with passion," she said, quoting the glib devil that had control of her tongue.

Judd unsnapped the front catch of her bra. "I don't want to go back either," he said.

"But you told them we'd drive them back, didn't you?"

The pointed tip of his moist tongue followed the scalloped lace of her bra. His chin nuzzled the obstruction aside. "Let's not talk; let's make love. I want you, my love, my wife."

"You aren't listening to me," she protested. "I don't want—"

The ornery devil inside her began to fade in a mist of licking flames spreading from the rosebud tips of her breast, which tautened beneath her husband's convincing argument. Laura Lee felt her traitorous body respond. Desperately she willed herself to revolt against his masterly touch. With a will of their own her fingertips began massaging the tense muscles of his shoulders and neck.

How could she think straight when his dark

hair felt so good, when his lips sent shivers down her spine, when he kissed her with such devotion? The smell of his aftershave mingled enticingly with the clean fragrance of his hair. Laura Lee groaned.

"Tell me you need me as much as I need you," Judd whispered, his voice thick with love.

Winning or losing dropped by the wayside. With slow, lazy strokes he unlocked the inner core of passion she had sought to conceal. The magic, the pulse-quickening excitement of loving and being loved stole any thoughts of being lucid from her mind.

"I do," she panted. "I do need you, want you."

Laura Lee heard the taint of triumph in his low, throaty groans; she saw the bright fire of victory shining from his brown eyes, but his mouth, hungrily biting her lips, sipping at her tongue, destroyed any rebellious thoughts. Tomorrow, when the brightness of the sun allowed clarity of thinking, she would rebel.

CHAPTER EIGHT

Laura Lee watched Judd sleep. *How I love him,* she mused. Her sleepy eyes strayed down his chest and flat belly to the strip of white flesh the sun hadn't touched. *Tomorrow arrives stealthily,* she mused, watching the sunlight dispel the shadows in their room.

At dinner, a hairbreadth away from scandalous behavior, she should have gracefully agreed to take Mac and Vanessa back. They'd make the remainder of their honeymoon miserable if they stayed. In the middle of the night she had made a fervent resolution. She wouldn't fight returning to Kansas City.

Today would mark a dramatic change. She would readily agree to going home, but there would be stipulations.

Once again Judd had established a pattern Laura Lee knew she couldn't live with. They had joked about it, seriously discussed it, and dropped it as unimportant. But it wasn't. Anytime Judd couldn't convince her with logic, he seduced her with passion.

"Good morning, love," Judd whispered. He snuggled closer to her curved form and lightly kissed her cheek.

"We're going home today, cutting the honeymoon short, aren't we?"

There wasn't any point in delaying the inevitable.

"Our honeymoon will never end," Judd said. "Anytime we're together, we'll be on our honeymoon. It isn't a time or a place; it's you and me, together."

The early-morning bristle of his dark beard scraped against the sensitive skin below her ear as he pulled her more closely into his embrace. He nibbled on the lobe of her ear with his front teeth.

"Okay," Laura Lee said readily. "I'll pack."

"Okay?" Judd seemed shocked by her quick capitulation. "You don't mind?"

After swinging away from him and off the side of the bed, she crossed to the bathroom. Acting as though she couldn't care less about the fate of their honeymoon, she squeezed toothpaste on her toothbrush and began brushing her teeth.

When she glanced up, Judd was leaning against the doorjamb, peering at her as though she had completely lost her mind. Laura Lee gave him a foamy grin, then rinsed her mouth out. She extracted her hairbrush out of the travel case on the vanity and excused herself as she slipped past him.

"Wait a minute, Mrs. Simpson. Something isn't kosher. Why aren't you screaming and kicking?"

"Why fight the inevitable? You decided last night to take them back, didn't you?"

"I toyed with the idea of telling them to go to hell," Judd replied honestly.

He narrowed his dark eyes as he watched Laura Lee brush her auburn hair with short, choppy strokes. She appeared calm on the outside, but he knew her well enough to recognize the jerky motions as symptomatic of inner turmoil.

"But you didn't."

"No," he admitted. "I didn't. I wanted to discuss leaving with you and make a mutual decision."

A mixture of a laugh and a snort passed through her lips. "Judd, I've agreed to return. There's only one catch."

"What?"

Laura Lee turned around and faced him squarely. "From this point forward we will settle our disagreements outside the bed. In fact, for the next month you and I aren't going to make love until we manage to respond to each other like two rational adults instead of like randy teen-agers."

Tossing his head back, Judd roared with laughter. When he saw the look on her face, he swallowed his chuckles. "You are kidding, aren't you? You don't actually believe I'm going to return from my honeymoon and be . . . celibate?"

She answered his question with one of her own, imitating his incredulous tone. "You don't actually think I'm going to let you rule the roost from the bed, do you?"

"Now wait a minute," Judd protested. "You can't live with me without sex any more than I can be around you for more than five minutes without wanting to bed you."

Arching one eyebrow, Laura Lee denied his claim.

Judd turned away from her, feeling bruised. Hands on his hips, he strode to the balcony door. Could she turn passion on and off like a charcoal grill? he wondered. No, his ego denied it. Since the first time they had been together, she hadn't been able to keep her hands off him. *Well, my lovely bride, it's time you learned who can control their lust. Within a week you'll be begging me to "court disaster" again.*

"Okay," he agreed succinctly. "But I have a contingency of my own."

"Yes?"

"Since you're obviously bound and determined to follow through with this outlandish scheme to bring me to heel, and I frankly admit to being unable to win any verbal battle, we'll compromise. I won't make love to you for a month if you don't talk to me for the same period of time."

"But that's ridiculous! How can we discuss anything like rational adults if I'm not allowed to voice my opinion?"

"See? Already you're about to convince me that my stipulation is ridiculous and yours isn't. Care to go to bed right now and end this farce before it begins?"

"Judd Simpson, I can go without speaking longer than you can go without sex!" she retorted, her temper flaring.

"State nickname . . . Show Me." Judd grinned from ear to ear. She wouldn't be able to keep her mouth shut any more than he could keep from making love to her. The bargain was fair.

Laura Lee opened and closed her mouth in rapid succession. This wasn't working out the way she had planned. In the dialogue she had mapped out in her mind, he was supposed to see the logic in her reasoning. Where had she gone wrong?

"Can't do it, can you?" Judd asked with laughter bubbling below the surface of his voice.

Gray eyes narrowing, she tossed the brush onto the bed. She'd show him. He hadn't thought of everything on such short notice. There was a loophole somewhere, and she'd find it. Sticking her hand out, she indicated her willingness to shake hands, sealing the bargain with closed lips.

Judd signaled for her to wait a minute. Smiling, he opened a drawer, pulled out a pair of shorts, and put them on. Deliberately he turned toward her as he did so.

"Since you're determined to go through with this, I think there should be a prize for the winner. Should you win, as isn't likely, what would you like to have? But remember, make it easy on yourself. Whatever you choose, I'm going to think of something of equal value." He smiled. "I want to be fair."

Laura Lee pursed her lips and gave him an Archie Bunker raspberry.

"Very clever," Judd responded, laughing.

I'll show you clever, she thought angrily. Between thumb and forefinger she raised the diamond on the gold chain around her neck. She pointed to her ears.

"Diamond earrings? You're pretty confident of yourself, aren't you?"

Mutely smiling, she reached up and patted his cheek affectionately.

"Now what would I like to have?" Judd asked

147

the question aloud. He might as well get used to hearing only the sound of his voice. Who knows? he mused. She might slip if he provoked her enough. "New golf clubs? A fishing boat? A hunting trip? That's it! Next year, if I win, we go to the mountains on a hunting trip . . . all expenses paid by you."

Laura Lee's smile slid the other way around. She hated guns, and he knew it. But she couldn't protest without automatically losing. She stuck her hand out.

Shaking it, Judd smiled mischievously. "You forgot the first rule of debate. You didn't define the terms. Making love refers to the sexual act between a man and woman. I am, according to the bargain, not allowed to bed you. Correct?"

Laura Lee cautiously nodded her head, clamping her lips into a straight line. He was up to something. He was supposed to be grinding his teeth in frustration, not grinning as if a truckload of free food had been delivered to the restaurant.

"I'm restricted, but you aren't completely off limits." He closed the gap between them until their bare toes touched. His brown eyes filled with mirth, he leisurely traced the snowy white line her bikini made with his fingertips.

She opened her mouth to protest. The finger Judd laid on her lips kept her silent. It hadn't taken him long to find an escape clause. He could dilly-dally around all he wanted to as long as he didn't complete the act.

Two people could play that game, she deemed wickedly. She reflected his smile as she raised herself on tiptoe. Locking her hands behind his neck, she rocked gently against his body.

The smile faded from Judd's face when she flicked the lobe of his ear with her tongue. *Sweet, sweet temptation.* He moaned silently. *What have I gotten myself into?* He couldn't even kiss her without wanting to love her completely. Why didn't someone knock on the door? Why wasn't the telephone ringing? He needed immediate distraction, or he wouldn't be able to refrain from claiming what was his.

"Laura Lee, love, speak to me. Call this whole damned thing off." His fingers flexed into her flesh as he lifted her off her feet.

Stubborn as any Missouri-born mule, Laura Lee shook her head. She had double-dated on her honeymoon, had agreed to depart after two nights, but she wasn't about to mutter the first word regardless of how much she wanted him. Stepping away, she made a sweeping gesture toward the bed.

The contest of wills would have long-lasting repercussions. Judd realized that by seeking mutual pleasure, he would lose more than a pair of diamond earrings. She would be validating

149

her claim that he lacked control. Anytime she wanted to punish him, she would follow the tried-and-true rule other wives used: Withhold sex.

"Tell me you love me," he whispered in a strangled voice.

Laura Lee found her own escape clause. Proud of herself, she beamed him a wide smile. The commercial saying "If you want to be heard, whisper" crossed her mind. According to the terms of the agreement, she couldn't even whisper, but she could . . . "I love you," she mouthed without making a sound.

Judd slapped his forehead. "Great. That's just great! I can touch without feeling, and you can talk without saying anything."

Disgusted with himself, with Laura Lee, with their stupid agreement, Judd heaved the suitcase onto the bed. He wasn't going to beg her again. In the middle of tossing his clothes into the bag the phone rang.

Impishly Laura Lee touched his shoulder and pointed to her mouth.

"I'll get it," Judd growled, picking up the receiver. "Hello."

"Someone standing on your tail or do you always bark before breakfast?" Mac inquired jovially.

"What do you want?" Judd demanded impatiently.

"What's wrong? Is Laura Lee screaming bloody murder about leaving a little early?"

"No. She's remarkably quiet," Judd answered, tongue in cheek.

"You sound like you didn't get any last night, ol' buddy."

"Wrong again. As usual, every night is one to remember."

Judd wheeled around when Laura Lee tapped him on the shoulder.

"Don't discuss our love life with him!" she mouthed, shaking her fist angrily.

"Just a second, Mac." Putting his palm over the phone, he grabbed her flailing arm. "Speak up, dear. I can't hear you."

Opening her mouth wider, she repeated her message. Judd shrugged and turned back to the phone. There was more than one way to skin a cat. If she wouldn't voice her love, she might speak to him if he riled her enough.

"Yep. Laura Lee is the greatest," he was saying loudly and enthusiastically when out of the corner of his eye he saw her pick up her clothes and slam into the bathroom.

"Vanessa is all packed. When do we leave?"

"I don't recall giving you a definite 'yes' last night. Didn't I say I'd have to talk it over with my wife?"

Mac groaned into the receiver. "Ol' buddy, I'm going to have the shortest marriage on record unless we're out of here by noon. Laura Lee is a sport. She understands, doesn't she?"

"We'll be ready in an hour."

"Thanks, ol' buddy. I won't forget this."

Judd dropped the phone back into place. "And neither will my wife," he muttered. When he heard the toilet flush, Judd had the premonition that more than toilet paper was going down the tubes.

"That was the other 'happy couple,'" Judd informed her as he resumed his packing. "Do you want breakfast here or on the road?"

Silence.

He raised his voice an octave, trying to imitate her. "Oh, Judd, whatever you want to do is fine with me." Dropping back to his normal pitch, he responded, "But, darling, whatever you want is fine with me." He paused, then squeaked sarcastically, "Let's go to bed and discuss it."

Laughing, Laura Lee popped him on the rear end with a damp towel. "I'm finished in the bathroom," she mouthed.

"And I'm finished in the bedroom," he replied. The double entendre wasn't missed by his wife. He heard her tsk-tsk-tsk.

She pulled her clothes out of the dresser drawer. Was there a change in Judd's jaunty walk? she pondered when he passed by her. Usually he patted her rump or gave her a quick peck on the cheek anytime he was within a foot of her. Not this time. She could almost see the imaginary line he had drawn around her.

Laura Lee smiled. *By nightfall I'll have won myself a set of sparklers and proved my point. Judd might not like the stipulation, but he hadn't lost his sense of humor . . . and neither have I. Otherwise, we'll have more at stake than earrings and a hunting trip.*

The clothes Judd packed would have to be ironed unless she repacked them. There was only one thing she hated worse than rushing to the dryer when she heard it buzz, and that was having to iron the clothes if she left them in the dryer to get wrinkled. Now she had more clothes to be responsible for. She shrugged her shoulders, removing his wad. What had her friend Meredith said after she had been married for a short time? A woman gets married to have a man shoulder her problems and finds herself with two sets of dirty clothes instead of one.

Chuckling, Laura Lee mouthed, "Point taken, Meredith."

But right now she had a bigger problem than rumpled clothing. She had to make Judd aware of his solution to every problem, large or small. The corner of her mouth lifted fractionally. Of course, she silently admitted, teasing him with her body the way he verbally teased her could be as much fun for her as it was frustrating to Judd.

Before they were married, before they had gone to bed together, she had been careful to avoid any teasing situations. But now the ground rules had changed. Hadn't Judd bragged about his self-control? Hadn't he been certain he could avoid physical temptation longer than she could remain silent?

If Judd weren't going to abide by any rules, neither would she.

Finished with the repacking, she started to close the suitcase and halted. With swift, deft hands she removed her cotton T-shirt with the resort name blazing across the front and her bra. She stuck her head into the V neckline and waited until she heard the bathroom door open before she pushed one arm into one armhole and then the other arm into the second armhole.

Judd sucked air into his lungs to cool the fires he felt merely seeing her bare back. The effect of seeing his wife put on her clothes was more powerful than seeing a thousand women stripping. He rammed his clenched fist into the pockets of his cutoffs. "That's a dirty trick," he snarled.

She smiled cheekily as she turned around and lowered the front of her T-shirt with tantalizing slowness. His dark pupils immediately dilated. He could hide his desire behind a lopsided grin, but he couldn't control the involuntary reactions.

Judd watched her reply. She mimed being on the telephone. Holding her thumb straight, the other four fingers flapping up and down, she illustrated his dirty trick. Then she hung up the imaginary phone, pointed to her mouth, and began feeding herself.

He had to laugh and hold up his hands for her to stop. "Okay, okay, so I pulled a few dirty tricks myself."

Gray eyes twinkling mischievously, she shimmied her shoulders and walked toward him.

"Naughty, very, very naughty," he commented in a gravelly voice.

Her breasts swaying in rhythm with her slender shoulders fascinated him, mesmerized him. Before he knew what he was doing, his hands were out of his pockets, his fingers were circling the taut nubs of each breast.

"You don't intend to go braless, do you?"

A wicked smile on her mouth, Laura Lee nodded up and down.

He cupped the weight of her feminine flesh in the palm of his hand. "You're playing with dynamite."

After lifting the front of her shirt, she traced the letters he had tongued on her front: D-I-S-A-S-T-E-R. The tip of one reddish eyebrow arched toward the gentle waves of her hair, questioning his meaning.

"I would be courting disaster if I made love to you now. Much as I want to, I won't. Otherwise, you'll think you can control me via the bed."

Laura Lee pointed toward Judd, then toward herself, silently indicating she would be using his tactics of persuasion. She shrugged her shoulders, asking what the difference was.

The soft cotton fabric clung beneath her breasts when he removed his hands. The voluptuous bait tempted him. One more bobble of her breasts, and Judd knew the enticing snare would clamp shut.

"Put your bra on. You're not going out in public—"

A mutinous expression replaced the question mark. Lips pursing together, she shook her head. If his tongue could be his agile weapon, she wasn't going to disarm her arsenal.

"Do you have any underwear on?" Judd demanded.

Her lips curved upward as she caught his hand. *Find out for yourself,* she mutely told him.

Judd jerked his hand back as though burned on a hot grill. "You do. I can see the line." He desperately tried to change the subject.

"Are you ready to go?" he inquired softly,

tenaciously hanging on to the last shred of his self-control.

Laura Lee pertly answered with a toothy smile. She crooked her finger and beckoned him to investigate for himself.

"Yes, sweetheart, I am," he replied in a falsetto voice. "Follow me right to the gates of sweet hell."

Laura Lee grinned. He deserved a strong dose of his own medicine . . . and she was just the person to administer it.

Several silent hours later Laura Lee glared at her dear, sweet husband of two days. He had tried every trick in the book to make her talk. They couldn't leave the Ozarks without getting another memento, could they? There had been several wood carvings she would have liked to have had, but when she refused to voice a resounding "yes," Judd had shrugged and gone on.

Mac and Vanessa had gleefully joined the game. They were in high spirits. When they suggested that they all get together for dinner and the movies when they got home, Laura Lee had pinched Judd's thigh until she was certain it was black and blue, but her dear husband had glibly accepted, saying they didn't have anything else to do.

On the journey home Laura Lee had nodded

and shaken her head so often she felt as though her brain were coming loose.

"Want something to eat?" Judd asked once she had unlocked the front door to the house.

"I want to be carried across the threshold," she mouthed.

"Cat got your tongue? Can't hear a word you're saying."

Laura Lee tugged at his hand, pushing his shoulders down until he hunkered near the floor of the front porch. Smiling, she wrapped her arms around his wide shoulders and motioned for him to rise.

"I'll carry you over the threshold. All you have to do is ask," Judd muttered as he straightened to his normal height.

In slow motion, she made a slicing gesture across her throat, then thumped him on the chest. When he started to push past her, she grabbed his arm and held up one finger. Pulling her thumb back, she placed it beside her temple. She wiggled the top joint of her thumb up and down six times. Pointing to the ground, she kicked and stamped several times just for good measure.

Judd couldn't help laughing at her wild threats. To Laura Lee being carried into their home for the first time held the same special meaning the big wedding, the reception, and all the other traditional trappings contained. Much as he wanted to make her talk, he couldn't deny her this special moment, nor could he deny himself the privilege of being the man who held her in his arms as they entered their home together as husband and wife.

He swooped her high into his arms and planted a smacking kiss on her lips. Silently Laura Lee cuddled against him. She didn't say anything, but he could tell by the cloudy look in her gray eyes that she was happy he wasn't ruining this moment for her.

"I do love you," she mouthed solemnly.

With loving tenderness she rewarded him by melting her sweet, silent lips against his.

Judd fervently returned the kiss. She didn't have to lead him anywhere. They were home. They were married. They were still on their honeymoon. And Laura Lee had learned one lesson on their honeymoon: the spoken litany of love. Once he had begun making love to her, she wouldn't be able to remain silent.

"It's good to be home," he sang softly into her dainty ear.

Balancing on one leg, holding her close, he kicked the door shut.

CHAPTER NINE

Judd nipped at the soft, scented, ticklish skin along her neck. "Let's wash off the travel dust," he suggested, gently blowing near her ear.

Is that synonymous with taking a cold shower? Laura Lee questioned silently. As though her skin had been doused with the icy thought, goose bumps pricked on her skin. Was he going to dump her into the shower and join her?

An icy shower was the farthest thing from his mind. He carried her through the hallway, into the bedroom, past the inviting king-size bed, and into the bathroom. The single extravagance he had insisted on when they built the house was the design of the bathroom. It included twin marble vanities, a large shower, a sauna, and a giant Jacuzzi bathtub adorned with a golden swan that filled the tub. Mirrors surrounded the tub on three sides.

His fiancée had been too inhibited to play around in their private playpen. Confident her reticence had been shed since the vows had been taken, he released his hold on her silky, smooth legs and let her body slowly slide down until her sandals touched the fluffy bath rug.

"Care to share the tub?"

The bright light of curiosity glowed in her gray eyes. Lazily she lowered one eyelid in a seductive wink. Judd chuckled and quickly divested both of them of their summer clothing. After walking over to the sauna, he turned on the dial, keeping his eye on the mirrors as his wife stooped over to turn the gold-handled faucet.

Completely nude, he could see his manhood rising for the occasion. She wouldn't be able to refuse him once they were relaxed in their own home, soaking in the tub, would she? Judd grinned presumptuously, mentally predicting the outcome.

"I'll be right back."

Judd, naked as the day he was born but infinitely more virile, rushed out of the bathroom and into the kitchen. Whistling a jaunty tune, he removed a bottle of wine from the refrigerator and two wineglasses. Chuckling to himself, he knew all their problems were about to be resolved.

Seconds later he entered an empty bathroom. His happy-go-lucky whistling abruptly ended.

She wasn't where he had left her. Had she chickened out at the last minute?

"Laura Lee?"

From inside the sauna he heard a rapping response. A wolf whistle later, Judd stepped inside the dry heated cubicle with two glasses of wine. Laura Lee was stretched out on the lower bench. A thin film of perspiration already coated her pinkish skin.

"Gorgeous." He complimented her as he handed her a glass. "You've become a sexy, foxy lady."

Laura Lee had never felt so delightfully wicked. Smiling, she dipped her index finger into the cool wine and dribbled it on her lips invitingly. Judd bent at the knee, lowering himself to her level.

"Naughty"—the tip of his tongue met hers as they both claimed the nectar of the gods—"but nice!"

She made a low, purring noise in the back of her throat that affected the rising temperature in the room. As though she had grown claws especially for the occasion, she raked a path through the hair on his chest. Lips parted, she mouthed his name silently, enticingly pouting her lips.

With perseverance and singleness of purpose, he directed his lips and fingers toward her pliant, moist body. His perspiration blended

162

with hers, making a heady scent that filled his nostrils. She tasted as delicious as she looked and smelled. While she peppered tiny kisses across his shoulders, he tasted her neck, shoulders, breasts, and belly.

He had teased her about following her to the gates of hell, but he hadn't realized how pleasurable intense heat could be.

Lethargically, Laura Lee watched his head move lower and lower. The heat, the touch of his questing mouth made her feel as though the sun's rays had percolated through her veins. The heat became internal as well as external.

Droplets of sweat made erotic paths down Judd's spine. His dark hair became damp, clinging to her fingers when she increased the pressure against the back of his head. She could almost hear a lazy melody humming in her ears.

She opened her mouth to protest when Judd began nibbling at the inside of her upper thighs, but a warning bell pealed ominously. Judd hadn't intended to "wash off the travel dirt"; he had deviously plotted her downfall. Intentionally he had kept his body folded to restrict her hands from arousing him in reciprocation.

Fingers coiling, she pried his head upward. His brown eyes flowed over her like thick, sweet molasses. With his face flushed, he panted puffs of scorching air against her skin.

"Ready?"

Mutely Laura Lee shook her head, closing her firm thighs. With one hand she leaned over and picked up his wineglass. She fanned her face, then gestured toward the door.

Judd smiled. Her gray eyes were smoldering with concealed passion. She wanted him as desperately as he wanted her. As he rose to his feet, she intimately touched him. *Ah, yes, my lovely enchantress, take me home, make me yours.*

He pushed against the door with the sole of his foot. The cool air gushed into the heated room, condensing on their hot skins. Judd flicked the switch to turn on the Jacuzzi.

"Inviting?" he asked huskily when her eyes followed the sound of bubbling, splashing water.

Laura Lee gracefully moved toward the tub, arching her back as she pulled the long tendrils of damp hair off her neck.

In the mirror Judd saw the upthrust of her breasts. He slowed her ascent into the tub by wrapping his tanned arm around her waist. She leaned back against his chest, eyes closed, one foot on the side of the tub, the other still on the cool floor.

"You're the woman every man dreams of." He groaned as he splayed his fingers over her taut belly. "Creamy perfection against my darker skin. A beautiful dramatic contrast of light and dark, feminine and masculine, woman and man."

His hands lingered on each peak, each valley, the smooth, damp silkiness of her skin, the equally silky texture of her feminine hair. Laura Lee made low, growllike tones between his phrases. The certainty of the outcome was more vivid than the reflections in the mirror.

When he settled his hands around her waist and gently nudged her forward, she opened her eyes and stepped into the pool of frothy warm water. At first her hands held her auburn hair atop the crown of her head; then, listlessly, they lowered into the water.

Judd sat on the edge of the huge marble tub watching the ecstatic, serene expression on her face. The jetting water fluttered against the dusty rose-colored tips of her breasts. A blissful smile curved her lips upward.

Unable to watch without touching, he stepped into the tub and sank into the water. The water level raised to scant inches below her chin. Once seated, he bent his long legs and placed a kiss on each of her small toes before putting one of her feet, then the other, beside his waist.

With long, sweeping strokes his hands went from her ankle to her outer thigh.

"Are you humming, groaning, or calling my name?" he asked, his voice barely loud enough to carry over the sound of rushing water.

Laura Lee rocked her head against the side of the tub. "This is wonderful," she mouthed.

"You're being stubborn, love."

Her smile widened.

"Can you resist whispering my name when I touch you here . . . and here?" he asked coaxingly.

Clamping her lips tightly, Laura Lee concentrated on the soothing water, the melody humming, vibrating in her heart, and away from the erogenous zones Judd touched. They weren't in the bed, but Judd was using the same technique to defeat her. Yes, she was being stubborn, but mulish or not, she wasn't going to say a word until they intimately joined.

Frustrated by her silence, and nonparticipation, Judd clenched his back teeth together. His hands snaked around her upper arms as he slid forward. The impact of the sudden shift spilled water out of the tub. Her eyes batted open when water sloshed on her face.

Eyes widened, she used her wet hands to wipe the dewy drops of water from her eyes and lashes. The proof of how Judd's mind was working nudged against her. Victory gleamed in his brown eyes. *Trust me,* they said, beckoning, *talk to me.* Purposely, defiantly, she dropped her hands beneath the frothy water level.

Her eyes sent him a message he couldn't ignore: *You made the rules; break them.*

Once the message had been received, he reacted impulsively. He had tried everything, but . . . His strong hands wrapped around her ankles; he yanked them upward. Instantly her head dunked below the water.

Laura Lee inhaled at the wrong moment. Warm water swam into her nose and opened mouth. The unexpected dunking had resulted in an automatic reflex. She had clung tightly to the object in her hand. Before her head broke the surface, she could hear Judd's scream.

Coughing, she spewed water out of her mouth. In a watery blur she saw Judd hop out of the tub. Mentally she screamed, *That was a dirty trick!* But when she saw Judd jumping up and down, she didn't need to say a word. She pushed her auburn, tangled hair out of her eyes.

"That hurt," Judd yelled, grabbing a towel and gently patting his self-inflicted injury. "That was a lowdown stunt."

Bobbing her wet head up and down, she agreed.

"You're feeling smug, aren't you? You just about ruined our future family, and you're grinning. Have you no shame!"

She picked up the bar of soap out of the dish, ignoring his shouts, and began lathering her shoulders. Acting as though nothing out of the ordinary had happened, she hummed a wicked tune.

"It's a good thing I didn't try to seduce you in front of the fire. You would probably have burned the house down rather than call the fire department!"

Laura Lee grinned at his ranting and raving. Somehow, even when he was absolutely furious, he injected humor into his invective. Laughing aloud, she gurgled loudly as she sank into the tub.

"I'm leaving," Judd shouted. "I'm going to get out of here. You're crazy, you know. Stark, raving crazy. And it's contagious. You're making me crazy, too!"

She heard his threat but didn't take it seriously. He'd be back assaulting her senses, seducing her with soft words in an effort to win the bet. For a moment she had almost apologized for inflicting pain in a sensitive area, but now she was glad she hadn't. If he had truly been injured, he would have been writhing in pain instead of jumping up and down like a jack-in-the-box. His male ego, not his manhood, had been squashed.

Judd, heavy-footed, stamped from room to room in the house. The aching he experienced wasn't due to the impetuous yank he had received; nonetheless, he hurt. How she could take a mild-mannered, sweet-tempered guy like him and in two days reduce him to a raving maniac, he didn't know. But she was driving him crazy. He had to be—to have made such a ridiculous bet!

"I'm leaving!" he shouted toward the bathroom as he picked up the suitcase in the hallway and stalked back into the bedroom. "How are you going to explain to everyone why your husband walked out after two days of marriage? They won't blame me! They'll think something is wrong with you. Some incurable social disease!"

Judd knew he was babbling like the deranged idiot he had accused her of being, but he couldn't keep his mouth shut.

"I'll be the hero. You'll be the villainess in this scenario! Everyone will feel sorry for me and wonder about you. You'd better get out here and stop me."

He pounded on the lid of the leather suitcase when the latches wouldn't open. The inanimate lock popped open. "A locked suitcase is less stubborn than my mule-headed wife!"

Filmy lingerie, cotton sports outfits, lacy underwear were hurled through the air without direction. Judd left his clothes in there and snapped the lid shut.

"I'm giving you one last chance. Get out here and speak to me, or I'm walking out and never coming back."

Maybe she can't hear me. Judd fumed, swinging the suitcase off the bed and striding to the bathroom door.

"I'm leaving," he said threateningly, glaring at her ominously.

Laura Lee raised her hand and wiggled her fingers.

Judd felt as though the top of his head were going to explode. She was waving good-bye! *Well, I'll be damned.* Spinning around, the suitcase whacking first one wall, then the other, he noisily departed.

In the midst of Judd's tirade, Laura Lee was certain he was bluffing, but when she heard the front door slam, she wasn't so certain. Would he really leave?

"No," she answered aloud. "He wouldn't be making jokes if he were serious about permanently moving out."

She climbed out of the tub and picked up the towel Judd had dropped in his rush to vacate the premises. Giggling to herself, she toweled off. Judd had really blown his cool.

The mirror over the vanity reflected her glee. She had a right to be proud of herself. Judd had tried every dirty trick in the book, but she had resisted. For the first time she had stood on her own two feet instead of letting him walk all over her. Her self-esteem knew no boundaries. She had become Judd's equal.

Towel in hand, she strolled into the bedroom.

It appeared to have been struck by a capricious tornado. Clothes were strewn everywhere.

"I'll have to do a better job of training him," she said gloatingly. "If I can win the bet, anything is possible!"

But you haven't won. The devil inside of her tweaked her. Much as she hated to admit it, she hadn't won. Granted, she hadn't said a word, but they hadn't made love either. She flicked her bare shoulder as though ridding herself of the devil, which had managed to spoil her victory.

Several hours later her euphoria had dissipated completely. She had geared herself up for the final round in their battle of wills. Instead, she found herself alone, shoving medium-rare steak and frozen vegetables around a mound of potatoes. Judd hated steak and TV dinner types of vegetables. Knowing this, she had carefully planned the coup de grâce. Using a new strategy, she had plotted to infuriate him to the point where he would be pushed to hauling her into the bedroom and ending the battle.

Steak, her favorite meat, tasted like half-cooked shoe leather. The green peas, pebble-hard, contrasted in color and texture with the fluffy white potatoes that reminded Laura Lee of paper wads. She dropped her fork.

Where is he? she wondered. *Did he go back to his parents' house? To the restaurant?*

None of the options appealed to her. Wouldn't

his parents gloat if he showed up on their door-step? She could almost hear the sympathy ooz-ing from his mother. His father wouldn't side with her either. Hadn't they disapproved of her in the first place? They hadn't made any secret of their disappointment when she had flashed her engagement ring in their faces.

Laura Lee grimaced. She didn't want the em-ployees at the restaurant to know they were fighting either. Undoubtedly they would feed him a decent meal and listen to his accusations of having chosen a loony to live with.

How would she explain to her parents what had happened? She could just picture telling her mother Judd won all their arguments in the bedroom! She was certain her mother threw bread crumbs out the back door in the winter-time just in case a stork flew by with a new bundle of joy.

"Where are you, Judd Simpson?" she asked aloud.

The phone rang. Laura Lee despondently pushed her chair back, remembering they were supposed to eat dinner and go to the movies with Mac and Vanessa. In her list of "People I Don't Want to Know," she had forgotten the leading contenders. Vanessa would get her jol-lies off on this tidbit of gossip. Yet they might have some clue to where Judd had gone.

On the fifth ring she picked up the receiver.

"Hello?"

"Laura Lee? What are you doing home? You're supposed to be on your honeymoon." Her mother strung the questions together rapidly.

"How did you know someone would be here to answer the phone?"

"Your dad stopped by the Simpsons' restaurant, and he thought he saw your car going down the highway. We thought something might be wrong."

"Wrong? What could be wrong?" Laura Lee searched for a plausible reason to cut their honeymoon short. Unable to find one, she switched the topic.

"What was Dad doing at the restaurant by himself?"

"Well, uh . . ."

"Mom?"

"There was a bit of a problem at the reception and your dad went over to apologize. Did you have a good trip?" Laura Lee could hear the wariness in her mother's tone.

"Wonderful. What kind of problem? What is Dad apologizing about?"

"Why are you home early?"

"Mother . . ."

"Daughter . . ."

"Mac and Vanessa wanted to come home," Laura Lee answered truthfully.

"Where was Judd going? Why isn't he there with you?"

"Your turn to answer questions," Laura Lee said reprovingly.

She could hear her mother sigh deeply. Whatever had happened at the reception, she didn't want to talk about it.

"Your dad had some harsh words with Mr. Simpson."

"Why?"

"After the cake fell in, he called your dad to clean up the mess. Said the money we paid for the reception didn't cover disaster insurance." Mrs. Mason sniffed.

Laura Lee clenched her fist. "Dad should have punched him out."

"That's why he's over there apologizing. Mr. Simpson was laughing about the cake incident after you left. Your dad invited him out to the back parking lot."

Groan, groan, triple groan, Laura Lee thought. *Divorce courts, here I come.* Her father was eight inches taller and outweighed Mr. Simpson by forty or fifty pounds.

"They duked it out on the parking lot?"

"No. Mr. Simpson laughed." Mrs. Mason cleared her throat again. "Your dad refused to pay him. That's why he went over today. To give them a check."

"This has all the makings of a Hatfield-McCoy feud," Laura Lee commented.

"Your father wanted to straighten the mess out before you returned." Mrs. Mason laughed nervously. "He barely made it, didn't he?"

"Oh, Mom, I promised myself when I married not to be one of those women who run home right after the honeymoon, but I find myself digging through the closet, hunting for my track shoes."

"And I promised myself not to be one of those doting mothers who pry into their daughters' private lives."

Pausing, Laura Lee decided not to cry on her mother's shoulder. The problem was hers, not her parents'. She was no longer a toddler who held onto her parents' hands to keep from skinning her knees. She had to fight her own battles, solve her own problems.

"Is the honeymoon over?" Mrs. Mason asked softly, compassionately.

"Don't ask questions I can't answer, Mom." Laura Lee wasn't certain the honeymoon had begun, much less ended. "I'll call you."

After she had hung up, Laura Lee propped her elbows on the built-in desk and rubbed her forehead with shaky fingertips.

Judd slumped over the steering wheel, head resting on his forearms, fingers clamped around a small, square, velvet-covered box. The odometer had clocked off more than a hundred miles. He couldn't remember driving anywhere other than off the cul-de-sac he had nicknamed Lover's Lane when their house had been completed.

Less than two miles from the house he had pulled over to the curve to plan a face-saving strategy. Somewhere in the first ten miles while he had been silently berating his wife's stubbornness, he remembered the punch line of the old joke about a Missouri mule trainer. When the stubborn mule refused to budge for the new owner, the trainer had picked up a two-by-four and clouted it squarely between the eyes. "You have to get the mule's attention!"

Laura Lee hadn't used a broad beam, but she had gotten his attention. He realized he had tried to dominate her, using the missionary position. That's when he went to the jewelry store and bought a pair of small diamond earrings.

He ran his empty hand through his hair. Slumping backward, his thumb stroking the short nap of the velvet box, he closed his eyes. He remembered the first time he had seen Laura Lee. They both had been at a party at Lynda's house. Wintertime. Snow on the ground, a fire crackling in the fireplace, the men in the dining room playing poker, the women in the kitchen talking and laughing. The front door opened; Laura Lee, bundled in some sort of white fluffy fake fur, cheeks pink from the cold, arms full of firewood, entered. Wisps of auburn hair peeked out from beneath a saucy matching fur hat that resembled a snowball.

For the first time in hours Judd smiled. He'd been running a bluff then just as he had been when he stormed out of the house today. A pair of twos lost out to a pair of luminous gray eyes. The blue chips in the jackpot competed with his desire to introduce himself before some other male latched onto her. Excusing himself from the poker table, he had circled the room, the entire time keeping an eye on Laura Lee.

The moment she flashed him a cheeky grin he knew he'd won the jackpot. During the evening they had become acquainted. At midnight he offered to take her home. Politely but firmly she had refused. Disappointed but admiring her independent attitude, he watched her gaily wave as she departed.

When he called her the following day, she agreed to go out with him, but only if they double-dated. A double date? he recalled repeating. Safety in numbers, she had replied.

Laura Lee constantly surprised and baffled him. They were friends long before they became lovers. Shock must have been written on his face in bold letters the night he discovered her virginity. At twenty-six, beautiful, sexy, she should have had a rash of passionate interludes. But she hadn't.

"Romantically old-fashioned," he murmured.

Once they had made love, he expected her to push for a wedding date. She hadn't. In fact, she had refused to be hustled to the altar. She wanted a solid marriage based on a concrete foundation: a house.

Unaware at the time of what he was doing, he subtly began undermining her emotional foundation, her independence. The haywire doomed elopement, the reception at his parents' restaurant, the double-date honeymoon exemplified his attempts to subjugate her strong will. The unique trait that had attracted him initially he had repeatedly attempted to change.

Until now he hadn't been consciously aware of his desire to manipulate, to dominate her. Judd clicked the lid of the jewelry box. All that separated them at this moment was his false male pride. Much as he wanted to crawl back, beg her to forgive him, he knew humble pie didn't suit his palate. Was it possible to save face and still let Laura Lee know he wouldn't demand their decisions be made in the bedroom?

Judd racked his brain for a solution. Regardless of how furious she had been with him in the past, he could always count on one thing: her sense of humor. She'd been laughing when he walked out. Could he figure out a way to have her laughing when she opened the front door?

"I could call the furniture store and have them repossess the bed," he thought aloud. "Symbolically a great idea; practically it stinks."

The wheels in his mind began spinning. There had to be a simple solution. Judd cackled with laughter as an outrageous idea began forming. His brown eyes danced with mirth as he flicked on the ignition and revved the engine. *It might work*, he thought, chuckling. *It just might work.*

CHAPTER TEN

Laura Lee still had her hand on the phone when it began ringing again. Inwardly she dreaded answering it. How many people had recognized her car and seen Judd, alone, behind the wheel? Did the whole world know? Had he appeared on the six o'clock news?

"Simpson residence."

No response.

"Simpson residence," she repeated, louder. Shrugging, she started to hang up, but then she heard a strange noise. "Judd? Judd, is that you?"

Low, wheezy sounds came through the receiver, followed by a series of short pants.

"Is this an obscene phone call?" she demanded in a fake bored tone. "Sounds as if you need to go to a nose specialist."

Three snorts and a strangled gulp later Laura Lee banged the phone down. That's just what I need, the Mad Breather.

Immediately the phone began ringing again. She picked it up. "Look, you pervert. Call some other unsuspecting woman. My husband is a linebacker for the Kansas City Lakers. Want to snort in his ear?"

Judd chuckled. "Glad to hear your voice, love. I win, huh?"

"Where are you? Some sex maniac is—What do you mean, 'I win'? Telephone conversations don't count!"

"I'll be right home."

"You sneaky, dirty . . ." Laura Lee grinned. "I'll be waiting!"

In a mad dash, peeling off her clothes as she moved, she ran into the bedroom, giggling. Determined to be his equal in and out of the bed, laughing or crying, she slipped into appropriate clothing.

She barely had had time to tie the sash when she heard the front door open. Where had he called from? Next door? Fluffing her hair out from under the collar, she tried to keep a straight face as she walked toward the door.

Judd closed and locked the door when he saw his wife.

"Going somewhere?" he asked, his stomach sinking. "I brought you a peace offering."

"What makes you think I'm going somewhere? You're here . . . where you belong," she crooned in a teasing, lilting voice. She took the white medium-size box from his hands and set it on the foyer table.

"Why do you have your trench coat on if you aren't going anywhere?"

Laura Lee grinned impishly. "Can't have you being arrested for being the Mad Breather without your wife, the Wild Flasher, can we?"

Laughing at her audacity, he opened his arms. Laura Lee flung her arms around his neck and joined him with giddy, happy laughter of her own. In a rib-cracking hug, Judd swung her around and around joyously.

"I thought I'd have to slink under the door to get back in your good graces," he admitted. "I brought dinner. Humble pie for an appetizer and for a main course a heaping plate full of apologies."

"And for dessert?"

Judd grinned down into her gray eyes. "It's in the box."

Glancing over his shoulders she whispered, "Sweets?"

"Could be," he replied mysteriously. "Why don't you open the box and find out?"

"I'd rather stay where I am," she replied, snuggling closer into the safety of his arms. "You scared me."

He kissed her forehead lightly. "With my obscene phone call? It was my way of telling you I'd blown off enough steam. I wanted to come home."

"And the snorting?"

"Sucking fresh oxygen up to my brain so I can think clearly from here on out," he answered, loving the feel of her soft curves.

"But you won the bet, right? You're going to make me pay for a hunting trip."

Judd leaned back and ski-sloped his finger down her nose. After lifting her off her feet, he carried her to the sofa. "I didn't win anything."

"Neither did I," Laura Lee confessed. Her hands framed the thrust of his jaw. "The phone call didn't scare me as much as the thought of your not coming back."

"Not a chance." He winked one dark brown eye. "One of us has to stop being as hardheaded as a Missouri mule."

Laura Lee grinned, tracing the natural arch of his nearly black eyebrow. A mischievous light brightened her eyes. "I can prove I'm not a Missouri mule."

"How?"

"Mules can't reproduce. I can," she retorted smugly. "Guess you're the mule after all."

"Why did I ask? You always manage to win any verbal argument," he replied with a husky laugh.

"I win only when you let me." Laura Lee didn't want him under her thumb any more than she wanted to be under his. "I do owe you an all-expenses-paid hunting trip."

"And I owe you a honeymoon. Care to compromise?"

Hugging his neck, she replied, "I think I'm going to like being compromised."

"You're very, very naughty but also very, very nice. And extremely distracting," he added, unlocking her arms from behind his neck. "How do you feel about a long drive in a southerly direction? Just the two of us."

"To hunt ceilings?"

"And other wild things," Judd said teasingly. "I hear the Wild Flasher is on the loose and headed toward Florida."

"With her nefarious accomplice?"

"Um-hmmmm. Do you think I could get something to eat while you're packing?"

Remembering the mess in the kitchen, remembering what she had prepared for dinner, she squirmed on his lap. "Peanut butter and jelly?"

"Is that what you had for dinner? Now I really feel like a skunk. Good thing I brought something home with me."

"Judd Simpson, you purposely led me to believe the contents of that white box was a present for me!" *Distract him. Don't let him go into the kitchen.* "Why don't we check out the ceiling in the bedroom first?" she boldly suggested.

"Nope," Judd insisted. "I'm not going to be

accused of solving any problems in the bedroom. We're going to talk our way to Florida."

"I'll get some plates, and we can eat in here."

Laura Lee hastily swung her legs off the couch and scrambled off his lap. Judd caught her wrist.

"You're acting suspicious. What are you hiding in the kitchen?"

"Hiding? Me?"

"What did you do? Break all the dishes in a fit of temper?" Judd laughed as he lithely bounced off the sofa, grabbed the white box, and headed toward the kitchen.

Laura Lee stood immobilized. The moment he saw the steak, frozen peas, and instant potatoes, he would be furious. She could almost feel a wide white stripe painting itself down the center of her back. One Missouri mule reincarnated as a lowly skunk.

She covered her ears. The explosion would occur any moment now. Plates, silverware, pots, and pans would crash against the kitchen walls. She had promised, before they married, never to prepare any of those dishes.

"Laura Lee. Sweet, darling wife. Come into the kitchen . . . dear."

His voice lyrically crooned the words as though they were a marvelous new ditty he had spontaneously composed. Stiff-legged, she slowly, cautiously walked toward the kitchen.

Before entering the doorway, she called, "Judd, I know you hate steak."

"Yes, I do." He sang back.

"And frozen vegetables."

"Ummmm-hmmmm," he hummed.

"And mashed potatoes," she grumbled, feeling awful. "But remember, I fixed dinner while we were fighting. I was going to make you so mad you'd forget about winning the bet and—"

"And bodily cart you into the bedroom?" Judd stepped into the doorway. "Good plan. I'll have to remember it." He complimented her, spinning around and returning to the kitchen.

Laura Lee grinned. "I won't fix it again."

"I can always eat at the restaurant when my wife is feeling mulish," Judd quipped, refusing to get riled. "Come in and eat what I brought you."

Judd, a crooked smile on his face, stood beside the table with two plates and two forks in his hand. "Sit down."

"There's something else I think you should know."

"About our parents?" Judd guessed.

Laura Lee sank down into the cane-backed chair. "You know."

Pointing toward the white box, he replied, "I picked this up at the restaurant. Your dad had already been there. How did you find out?"

"Mom called."

186

"So? What's the problem?"

"Ever hear of the Hatfield-McCoy feud? A minor skirmish compared to the Mason-Simpson warfare."

"I don't recall vowing to love, honor, and obey anyone but you."

"But Dad—"

"Threatened to give my father a nose alteration? So what? His nose has been out of joint for months."

"It's me, isn't it?"

Judd pushed the plates and a knife toward his downcast bride. "Our parents feel the same way about each of us: I'm not good enough for you; you're not good enough for me. We'll have to prove them wrong, won't we?"

Nodding in agreement, Laura Lee started to open the box. "This is the first time we've really communicated with each other in months. I was afraid I'd lost my best friend by marrying him." Her head jerked up when she saw the contents of the box. It was the frozen tier of the ruined fruitcake. "We can't eat this!"

"Oh, yes, we can. Everybody says the first year of marriage is the roughest. We can't possibly go through anything rougher than our wedding and our honeymoon. We both are going to have a piece of our real wedding cake. We've earned it . . . early."

Laura Lee couldn't help chuckling. After

handing her husband the knife, she watched him cut two equal slices. It had thawed in the car. He leaned over the table and bite by bite hand-fed her one piece. Then he let her reciprocate. By the time she had mashed the last few crumbs on her forefinger and he had licked them off they both were broadly smiling.

"Ready for your first anniversary present?" Judd asked softly.

Laura Lee unbuttoned the first button on the lightweight trench coat. Although Judd's brown eyes flickered and shimmered, he reached into his pocket and withdrew a velvet box.

Two diamond earrings winked merrily at her when Judd raised the lid.

"Judd! They are beautiful, but . . . you won the bet, not me."

"No bet involved. Happy anniversary."

"I have something for you, too," Laura Lee whispered after she had given him a score of kisses.

"I'd rather talk," Judd said teasingly.

"No, you wouldn't. Follow me. It's something special."

Judd raised his hands as though he were giving up and said, "You won't hear any argument from me."

"It's in the living room."

"Wrong. Something special is here." Judd

didn't waste any time circling the table to lift his wife into his arms.

"I'm telling you, your gift is in the living room." She squirmed in his arms until he put her down. "Sit down on the sofa and I'll get it."

"Am I going to be as surprised as you were when you opened the rod and reel?"

Laura Lee opened the bottom drawer beneath the curio cabinet and took a deep breath. Some men wouldn't think much of the gift, but she hoped Judd would. She removed the rectangular package wrapped in silver paper, closed the drawer, and sat on the edge of the sofa.

"Happy anniversary, love."

He hadn't expected any gift other than her love. That would be enough for now, for a lifetime, for eternity. But when he removed the wrappings and gazed at their wedding invitation, sweetly centered in a lifelike bed of yellow roses and ribbons, he fully realized how much she loved him.

"You painted this, didn't you?" he asked reverently.

"Do you like it?"

"No, it's too precious merely to 'like.' It's a treasure." Slowly he raised his velvet brown eyes. "Diamonds don't compare with your gift of love."

"Diamonds are forever . . . and so is our marriage," Laura Lee whispered softly.

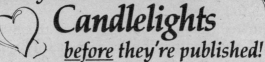

All-new Candlelight Newsletter

An exceptional, *free* offer awaits readers of Dell's incomparable Candlelight Ecstasy and Supreme Romances.

Subscribe to our all-new CANDLELIGHT NEWSLETTER and you will receive—at absolutely no cost to you—exciting, exclusive information about today's finest romance novels and novelists. You'll be part of a select group to receive sneak previews of upcoming Candlelight Romances, well in advance of publication.

You'll also go behind the scenes to "meet" our Ecstasy and Supreme authors, learning firsthand where they get their ideas and how they made it to the top. News of author appearances and events will be detailed, as well. And contributions from the Candlelight editor will give you the inside scoop on how she makes her decisions about what to publish—and how *you* can try your hand at writing an Ecstasy or Supreme.

You'll find all this and more in Dell's CANDLELIGHT NEWSLETTER. And best of all, *it costs you nothing*. That's right! It's Dell's way of thanking our loyal Candlelight readers and of adding another dimension to your reading enjoyment.

Just fill out the coupon below, return it to us, and look forward to receiving the first of many CANDLELIGHT NEWS-LETTERS—overflowing with the kind of excitement that only enhances our romances!

Candlelight
Ecstasy Romances™

$1.95 each